A Matter of Choice

Gail McAllister

Copyright © Gail McAllister

Cover Design by Vi McAllister

All rights reserved. No part of this publication may be reproduced, stored in a retrieval system, or transmitted, in any form or by any means, electronic, mechanical, photocopying, recording, or otherwise, without the prior written permission of the publisher.
Printed in the United States of America.

ISBN: 978-1-935920-05-2

About the Author

Gail McAllister, author of *Cry of the Sea Gull*, has a Masters Degree in Curriculum and Supervision and taught eighth-grade math and science before accepting a position in administration. Mother of two grown sons, she lives with her husband in the northern part of Wisconsin.

Dedication

With love for my sons,
Robb and Dave, and my husband, Clarke.

Chapter 1

Although the morning had begun with a clear, blue sky, an increasing cloudiness promised a rapid change and a rare fulfillment of the forecaster's prediction, assuring Cory Redlam that he would be walking in rain by the end of the day. They had been on the road for six hours and just when Cory decided that the driver of the eighteen-wheeler either had no tongue or forgot that he had picked up a passenger, he suddenly spoke.

"Football I bet, huh? Not heavy enough for a lineman. Tall, though. Quarterback?"

"What?" Cory asked, puzzled by the unexpected speech.

"You're in high school, right? Figured a big guy like you played football," the driver explained.

The common assumption that he played football made Cory wince inwardly. "No. I've never been interested in the sport," he said, ignoring the expression of disbelief on the driver's face.

Silence returned.

There was no point in explaining. One look at Cory Redlam's seventeen-year-old, athletic build and every person he ever met automatically assumed he played football. What was so great about football? He found no thrill in winning and, to the astonishment of everyone, he thought the game was a silly waste of energy.

With this point of view, the person he hurt most was his father, a man who had not only excelled at football but had been at the top of four other sports as well. In a nutshell, this was Cory's major problem. For at least the last ten years, he was the biggest disappointment of his father's life. Even the death of his mother when he was five, did not appear to devastate his father as much as the illuminating moment when he realized that Cory would never play sports—by choice!

In truth, he had played EVERY sport from the very minute his hands had grown large enough to hold the ball, the racket, the club, the bat, or the hockey stick. His father had trained him well in each and every sport, coaching with demanding discipline and rigorous workouts. To his father's immense satisfaction, Cory appeared to be a natural in everything he tried. But when Cory was finally eligible to play in organized sports, he simply refused to join a team or play the game when the only purpose was to win. It was Cory's belief that anything you spent hours perfecting, ought to be enjoyed. In every other regard he had done what his father wanted—good grades, decent behavior, and even learning the skills of each sport, but no more. It was time he made his own choices. And HIS choice was MUSIC!

The change of speed as the driver brought the eighteen-wheeler to a stop on the shoulder of the road shook Cory's attention back to the present. Peering through the rain-soaked window, he noticed how dark it had become and felt a moment of worry, knowing he still had a long way to go.

"Sorry, son. This is as far as I can take you. That's your road if you're sure you have the right number," the driver said, doubtfully. "I can't take the rig down a gravel road and I got a schedule to keep. Besides, I'm really not supposed to pick up hitchhikers anyway."

Quickly slipping into his rain parka and grabbing his sixty-pound hiker's backpack, Cory thanked the driver and stepped into the rain and darkening sky.

The cabin he hoped to reach before dark was probably thirteen miles from the highway and although his father owned it, no one had been there for at least ten years. When he was very little, his parents had frequently taken him there on vacation, but after his mother died, they had returned only once. As young as he was, Cory understood the pain his father felt and he accepted the choice to never return.

Now he reviewed all those memories as he trudged the wet and sandy logging road. Looking up at the towering pines, he drew in a deep breath and savored the smell of the trees and the damp, musty underbrush. The drips of rain, the occasional snap of a twig, the muted rustle of leaves as little creatures began to bed down for the night, were the only sounds of the forest. The chances of a car traveling this seldom-used road in a national forest were slim and Cory was sure he would be alone as he walked. Wisely, he had packed food, simple camping equipment, and clothing along with a few medical supplies to start his three months of freedom.

In the last twelve years, Cory had learned to do the cleaning, the cooking, the laundry and all the other chores that his mother would have done. Since his dad traveled internationally, sometimes for months at a time, he had done quite well in taking care of himself and in the process turned into an organized and self-disciplined young man. Well, maybe "man" wasn't the proper word. Didn't his dad always accuse him of NOT being one just by implying that you WERE a man, ONLY by playing football?

Shaking these disturbing thoughts from his mind, Cory shifted the heavy pack on his back as he continued down the center of the road. Reaching back over his shoulders, he re-tightened the straps that held his most treasured possession—his guitar, hanging upside-down in a waterproof case from the top of his backpack.

Coming upon the first fork in the road momentarily confused him, but calling on everything he could remember, the left fork seemed most likely. Things had changed in the ten years. Simple rock formations and some small ponds which Cory remembered from his childhood were now covered by underbrush or hidden by large trees. He had hoped to use them as guides but was forced now to travel by guess or intuition.

Worry began to seep into his thoughts when he checked his watch and again took the left path at the next fork in the road. He had only about an hour-and-a-half of daylight remaining, due, in part, to the overcast sky. Shaking the beaded water from his baseball cap, Cory tucked his thick, blond hair under it to keep as dry as possible and quickly increased his pace. Even in broad daylight the cabin would be difficult to find. Now, under these conditions, it would be an even greater challenge.

Five hours after he left the trucker at the highway, Cory stepped off the sandy, narrow road, having spied a rusting gate in the thick brush on the east side of the ditch. Had he not remembered the gate, nor been looking for it, he would never have noticed the iron bars, camouflaged by age and the surrounding growth. It would be natural to assume that the gate guarded a road or path, but only when Cory's feet felt the indentations of old car tracks under the tall grasses and small saplings that had grown over them, did he know that he was traveling in the right direction. Pulling out his flashlight, he picked his way by feeling with his feet for the barely perceptible tracks, pushing saplings out of the way as he went. Nearly a mile into the woods, Cory finally spied the log cabin in a small, grassy clearing surrounded by thick forest.

While he stood at the door of the cabin trying each of a half dozen keys from his pocket, Cory was overwhelmed by the incredible silence. No sounds from cars, people, planes, machinery, sirens, whistles, or horns could be heard. No motor boats, trains, factories or any other vibrations of humanity! Only SILENCE and an occasional drip of rain! Then, just when he was deciding to sleep on the porch rather than break in, the last key opened the lock.

The passage of time had clearly invited all manner of tiny creatures to invade the premises. While leaves, bark, twigs, grass, sand, and even acorns littered the porch, the remnants of ants, spiders, wasps, mice, and their droppings, along with dust, dirt, and sand covered everything inside.

Too tired to care, Cory slid his pack to the floor, carefully removing the guitar case and hanging it on a hook near the door before crawling up the ladder to the loft and dropping onto the first mattress he found.

Morning arrived with a deep drop in temperature, not uncommon to early June. Stretching, with his arms flung above his head as he sprawled on the mattress looking out the loft window, Cory could not help smiling. Yesterday's warmth and rain had saturated the air and the sudden drop of below-freezing temperature had painted the world with frost. It was beautiful! Brushing off the dried remains of bugs that had covered the mattress and now clung to his clothes, he rubbed his cold hands together to return circulation, and then began a thorough examination of the interior of the cabin.

Although there were three beds in the loft, only one of the mattresses could be used, and luckily it was the one on which he had slept. Mice had nested in the soft batting of the other two, leaving a shredded surface, lots of mouse droppings, and huge urine stains.

On the first floor of the cabin one large space served as both kitchen and living room with a potbellied, iron stove standing out from the northeast corner. Next to it, a bin of firewood flanked a short door leading into what once would have been a summer kitchen, now used as storage. There were dishes, utensils, pots, pans, towels, and bedding on shelving in the kitchen and an old wood cook-stove.

Built by a logging company when the first-growth timber had been removed from the area, the cabin was meant to be a primitive dwelling for weekend get-aways and as a vacation spot in the summer or a hunting shack in the fall. But Cory's quick appraisal told him that the place was in better shape than he had first thought and a thorough cleaning would improve things greatly.

As he surveyed the interior, he resolved to turn the cabin into his home for the summer. Home! Well, what was one more disappointment for his father when he arrived home from his business trip and found Cory gone? They had argued so much lately that maybe his father would only feel relief.

"You play football your senior year and I guarantee you'll get an athletic scholarship for college," he had shouted while stabbing his finger in the air at Cory.

"What's wrong with a music scholarship, Dad?" Cory had shot back.

Gritting his teeth and gathering as much control as possible his father had carefully replied, "Because your skill is in the area of sports, son."

"You have no idea, Dad, what my skills are," Cory responded as he had turned and walked away. It was never worth explaining. Although Cory had tried repeatedly to define and justify his desire to play classical guitar, all his father ever heard was the word "classical" which brought forth immediate contempt. Not only did he reject the idea, he labeled it cowardly. Only whimps and sissies played classical music and as far as judging Cory's ability, his father had never even heard him play. In fact, he wasn't sure his dad even knew that he had a guitar.

Cory shook the disturbing scenario from his thoughts. Right now, he needed some food, some water, and lots of energy to clean up the place—with the water taking first priority. By the time he stepped onto the deer trail that headed south from the cabin, Cory was wet to his knees from the melted frost on the tall grass. A brilliantly clear sky and lots of sunshine would quickly increase the temperature for a warm afternoon and he was soon humming one of his favorite tunes, swinging a large pail for the water he hoped to find.

Having been only five when he was here before, his memory of water was confusing. At first he pictured a large lake and then vaguely a small stream or creek. In either case, he knew his memory of water not far from the cabin was accurate. When he had gone no more than a quarter of a mile, the path widened and it was obvious from all the tracks, that animals had been there. The stream had poorly-defined edges and Cory found himself in muck before he realized it, but by stepping on rocks and fallen logs he was able to scoop a large bucket of clear water.

It took all day to haul the two mattresses out onto the lawn, sweep the cabin of debris, and wash all the surfaces with the water that had been proudly heated on the wood cook-stove in the kitchen. Meals consisted of dried fruits and nuts which Cory had wisely packed to get him through the first days. The two bottles of water he had brought, lasted only through the morning. Now he carefully sampled the water from the creek that he had boiled to make it drinkable.

With a large sickle, Cory cut as much of the grass and saplings as he could around the immediate perimeter of the cabin. After returning from the creek this morning, he had removed a dozen or more wood ticks from his clothing and he recalled that this would be the peak of the season for ticks—the enemy of the moment. Keeping the grass short would be a challenge, but it would also keep the ticks at a distance.

The evening was warm and the sun set quickly behind the woods at the west end of the clearing while Cory strummed his guitar as he sat in an old rocker on the porch. He hummed quietly to the tune he was playing and thought about his dream to attend a music school. By the end of summer, or sooner if his father found him, he had a choice to make. Play football his senior year and his father would support his college education. Refuse, and he would struggle on his own to improve his music and fight to earn a living in the music world doing what he loved. What made the decision all the more difficult was the fact that Cory really was a great football player. His throwing skills were unbelievable and every coach he met badgered him to play on a team. Now frustration swept through his weariness and with vigor he switched from strumming to picking the tune, "Bolero," loudly flaunting the Latin rhythm and his ability to play it.

The first signs of daybreak were already visible at four-thirty when Cory slipped out of his warm bed to skip across the ice-cold floor and light the kindling he had prepared in the potbellied stove the night before. Quickly he threw on his clothes and, placing a log on the infant fire, he grabbed his bucket and headed for water.

He lingered at the creek only a few minutes, drawing in the sweet smells of early morning and checking to see if any fish were visible in the slow-moving stream. Last night's stew, reconstituted from his dried-food supply, had been delicious, but he knew that the rest must be saved for any future emergency. Cory had two choices—walk all the way back to the highway and hitchhike to the nearest grocery store or eat off the land. While he preferred the second choice, he was aware of the challenge it would be to capture or locate food in the wild, especially with his limited knowledge and skills.

In the process of cleaning the cabin two shotguns and a rifle had been found in very good shape in leather cases behind a cabinet in the old summer kitchen. But Cory had never shot a gun. Although the memory was vague, he thought his parents had both once been involved in sport shooting. That would explain why the guns were here and Cory had never been taught to shoot. Some memories needed to be forgotten.

Half way back to the cabin he smelled the smoke from his stove and knew that he had been successful in making his first fire. However, when he stepped into the clearing, he saw that the smoke was billowing, not from the chimney, but from every crack and door or window of the cabin. Dropping the pail, Cory ran to fling open the cabin and grabbing the loft's ladder he rushed outside to slam it against the building. Over the years, birds had obviously nested under the chimney cap and the accumulated debris now blocked the smoke from escaping.

By the time Cory had the fire drawing properly, the day had warmed enough to let it die out and he simply laughed at his foolishness in not having checked the chimney first. While leaving the cabin doors and windows open to exhaust the smoke, he cut another patch of lawn with the sickle and cleared the debris from around the outhouse and a small garage-like shed that stood just opposite the cabin. Twice he stopped and stood perfectly still when he thought he had seen movement on a two-foot-high berm that ran from the outhouse to the creek trail. Finally, he went to investigate and from a distance of three feet, the whole berm appeared to be moving. SNAKES! The entire berm squirmed with the movement of grass snakes.

Along with the warmth of mid-morning, came several other surprises. On one of his many trips into the woods with a shovelful of berm and writhing snakes, he stumbled upon a wild turkey nest. Reasoning that it could not be into its incubation period yet, since it held a mere three eggs, he took them. Maybe finding your own food would be easier than he thought. The second surprise was not as pleasant. Two of the snakes, in their frenzy to escape the wrath of Cory's shovel and the disappearing berm, had slithered into the open cabin and were basking in a patch of sunlight on the floor just a few feet from the front door when he entered.

By noon the day's events had convinced Cory that he deserved a break from his work and pocketing his compass and pedometer, he struck out on a straight line to the north of the cabin. If he planned to live here all summer, it was necessary for him to have a broad picture of where the cabin lay in regard to the sprawling national forest. This afternoon he would trek for several miles to the north, mentally placing any notable trees or land formations into the gridwork he held in his mind. The pace was extremely slow the moment he left the clearing, stepping over fallen trees and around the areas of too-dense brush. Constant reference to the compass told him that he was still moving northward and an occasional check of the pedometer roughly informed him of his distance. At four o'clock, Cory checked his pedometer again and estimated that he had picked his way through only five miles of forest. It was at that moment that he first heard the grunt.

Standing motionless, he tried to determine from which direction the sound had come. Angry with himself for not having brought a weapon of some kind, Cory slowly inhaled deeply and noted, however, that he smelled no strong odor to suggest a bear, and yet, that might only mean that it was upwind and maybe HE, instead, could smell Cory. While shifting his eyes slowly to encircle the spot where he stood, another sound came from his right. This time, it was more of a moan and sounded more human than animal. Taking a chance, Cory shouted.

"Hey! Is anybody there?"

"Over…here!" came a muffled reply.

Picking his way toward the sound, Cory pushed aside the heavy underbrush that had been allowed to flourish beneath the short and scrubby trees of this area. "Keep talking so I can find you," he yelled.

"I'm…pinned down. I…need…help!" The voice was strained and unclear. "Over…ugh…here…"

On the other side of an unexpected outcropping of huge boulders, some as high as twelve feet, the terrain changed dramatically. Here tall trees with very little underbrush dominated the landscape. Letting his eyes sweep the area, Cory spied a fallen tree where he found the source of the moan

"Are you hurt?" he asked as he crouched at the head of a prone figure lying face-down on the ground.

From that face, smeared with dirt and dried pine needles, the eyes that looked up at him were the most beautiful he had ever seen. To his great surprise, they were the eyes of a woman. In a brief moment, he watched surprise, fear, and confusion appear and then fade from her face. Raising herself on her elbows as she lay on her stomach, she tried to brush the dirt off her cheeks.

"Believe it…or not," she said with a smile, "I'm not…hurt, just pinned down…and, from this position, it's…impossible for me to free myself. Can…you help me?"

Finding his tongue, Cory nodded and mumbled, "Sure!"

Her right foot was wedged in a small hole and a thick branch of a fairly large tree was caught across the back of both knees. Had she been on her back, she might have gotten herself free but the awkward, face-down position defied escape. Quickly freeing her, Cory stepped aside while she rubbed the circulation back into her feet and legs.

Although she had to be nearly sixty years of age with hair hanging down her back in a single, long braid that was the color of snow, her body was lean and athletic. Cowboy boots, denim jeans, and a plaid shirt with sleeves rolled to the elbow made her look like she had just stepped off a movie set. But her face was the most striking. Bright blue eyes, highly-defined cheekbones, small nose, and full lips still testified to the beauty she once held.

"Thank you," she stated simply as he helped her to her feet. "I'm Annie Winters."

"Hi," Cory answered, suddenly feeling shy and foolish. "Cory Redlam," he said, as he shook her extended hand.

"Well, Cory Redlam, I owe you. Anytime you ever need help, you can call on me. My place is about 300 yards that way." she said, pointing to the northeast.

It was difficult to shift his gaze from her face. Even the smudges of dirt did not detract from her beauty. "Well, um…I have to go about five miles south before dark, so if you're sure you're all right, I better start back," he stammered lamely.

With a smile on her face, she simply nodded.

He turned to go, knowing that she watched him as he picked his way through the woods. What was the matter with him? He had acted like a scared little boy; so afraid that he couldn't speak. And what was a woman like that doing in the middle of the forest? How had she gotten trapped and why hadn't he asked? Was she alone?

Maybe he should have offered to see her safely back home instead of leaving her standing there in the middle of the woods.

It took a great deal of concentration to forget about her and keep his mind on his direction of travel in order to retrace his steps. He was still agonizing over his foolish behavior when he suddenly realized that he had back-up in case of an emergency. Someone else was living within reach of his cabin. The thought was rather nice and as he neared his clearing, Cory decided that the day had ended slightly better than it had begun.

The peace of the late evening, however, was broken by the sharp ringing of Cory's cell phone, which he was recharging at the moment from his hand crank radio while he read by candlelight. The call was expected since Cory's dad had the habit of checking in with his son every other day. And thanks to the mobility of cell phones, his dad would never know that the call was being answered in the middle of a national forest.

With little to say, the call was short. They each reassured the other that they were fine and eating well. Both avoided the subject of football. Cory said good morning to his father in India, and his dad said good night to Cory half a world away.

Chapter 2

When Cory arrived at the cabin three days ago, his backpack carried as much dehydrated food as possible—oatmeal, stew mixes, nuts, dried fruits, and other items. Since he had no refrigeration, he brought only those perishables that he would consume within the next few days. Realistically, he accepted the possibility of running out of food, but with careful planning, and setting aside the rest of his supply for any potential emergency, his chances of making it through the summer were pretty good. Now, however, it was necessary to start "living off the land."

Among the old magazines and books that filled the bookcase under the cabin's front window was a survivor's guide listing edible, native plants. The accompanying pictures did much to convince Cory that one of the plants he had seen along the creek was indeed water cress. Along with the now confirmed dandelion greens and wild asparagus which he had seen among the tall grasses of the field on the north side of the cabin, Cory began to picture the gourmet meal he would feast on this evening.

Taking a rod and reel and some flies that he had discovered in the old shed next to the outhouse, Cory struck out for the dew-covered path to the stream where he was determined to catch the entree for his dinner. On his frequent trips to get water, he had noted the presence of a number of small fish and freshwater crabs or crawfish. The biggest hindrance to his imagined feast would be the manner of preparation.

Moving as quietly as possible with the awkward items he carried, Cory arrived at the stream in time to see a young doe lift her head from the water's edge and bolt into the tall reeds that lined the shore.

After three hours of snagging and losing the flies, Cory switched to worms on a hook. When that proved to be as inefficient as the other method, he trudged back to the cabin for two wire food strainers which, when placed in strategic positions in the creek, netted four fish in the next thirty minutes. It's all a matter of skill he thought proudly as he carried the strainers filled with fish and water cress back to the cabin.

The entire afternoon was devoted to Cory's garden. An old coffee can, found in the bottom of a trunk in the summer kitchen, contained a dozen or more half-used packages of garden seeds and with incredible hope, Cory dug up a narrow strip of lawn along the length of the south wall of the cabin to plant corn, beans, peas, and carrots. Collecting a large number of uniform tree branches, he cut them to five foot lengths and pounded them into the ground as a fence around the open side of the garden. Sharpening the top of each branch and weaving some rope through them resembled the forts of the old west. Cory was sure that no deer could possibly jump into such a narrow space.

Thinking he had examined every tiny cubbyhole, drawer, and shelf in each of the buildings on the property, Cory was continually amazed at the new things he found. His arsenal of precious tools expanded to include a shovel, rake, hammer, saw, screwdriver, pliers, level, and a cache of nails, screws, nuts, bolts, and other unidentifiable objects from a small tin box under one of the beds. There was even an old, manual lawn mower in the corner of the shed under an old piece of tarp. Although he was not particularly adept at handiwork, having the right tools would certainly help his efforts.

The day was ending hot and humid with a steady breeze from the south. Had Cory's radio not told him, he would still have known. A storm was coming. He could smell it in the air. As the sky darkened, he sat in his usual spot on the porch and played his guitar.

He loved the sounds and smells of the woods. He felt proud of his ability to live on his own, but to his surprise, he missed the sound of another voice—another human with whom he could share his hopes, feelings, and worries. He thought of Annie. She had taken him by surprise and he had reacted foolishly. Normally he handled himself remarkable well with adults. While he had many friends his own age, when he spent time with his father, it was usually with other adults, both men and women. Why had he felt so silly with her?

Although Cory had been well aware of the impending storm, the actual rain caught him off guard, so deep in thought was he. By the time he put away his guitar, closed the shed, and pulled the rocking chair into the cabin, thunder and lightning had added to the onslaught of wind and rain.

For two days, cooler weather was joined by a constant drizzle of rain following the initial storm which left leaves and branches flung all over the yard but actually did no serious damage. Cory spent the dark and depressing days restlessly practicing his guitar, fixing a broken chair, and building the framework of a dock for the stream. He'd fallen in twice when balancing himself on rocks or tree trunks while trying to fish. And fishing was his main source of food!

Common sense also told him that he needed to learn how to shoot the two guns he'd found, not only for the sake of defense, but ultimately to hunt small game for food. While his interest in guns was strong, the desire to kill was non-existent. But starving would certainly change his attitude.

When the weather pattern finally broke and the warmth and sunshine returned, Cory resolved to learn about guns. Taking the lighter, smaller rifle first, he pinned leaves to the side of the shed and backed away to load. Aiming carefully, he pulled the trigger. To his surprise, the small bullet neither knocked him down, nor did it make a very loud sound and to his disappointment, he could not find where the bullet had hit the shed. Three more attempts produced the same results. A trip completely around the shed, however, revealed that the bullets must have gone through the glassless windows on both sides because there they were, buried in the wall of the outhouse. Backing nearly to the edge of the clearing, Cory tried again. This time, although he missed all of his targets, he, at least, hit the shed.

The 12-gauge shotgun proved to be quite different. It took several tries in order to appreciate the shorter range and immense power of the single-shot. The first attempt slammed the gun against his shoulder and nearly knocked him off his feet, causing him to stagger backward. Not one to give up, Cory soon discovered that there was almost no recoil if he held the gun tightly against his body and leaned forward slightly. Confidently, he decided it was all a matter of practice.

While on his way back to the cabin with his arsenal of weapons, Cory's cell phone startled him. It was always with him when it wasn't recharging while hooked to his hand-crank radio. Hurriedly setting the guns down, he pulled the phone from his pocket.

"Hello?" he said tentatively. Who would be calling him now? His dad always called at night here, when it was early morning there.

"Cory, this is Dad," a voice responded, "Where are you?"

"Dad! Where are YOU?" Cory asked with rising panic.

"I'm here in India. But where are YOU?"

"What do you mean, where am I? You mean where am I standing at the moment? I'm outside. What's wrong, Dad? Are you feeling OK? How come you called at such a strange time? It's noon here. It must be the middle of the night where you are. Are you sure you're all right?"

Cory's bombardment of questions would surely guide the conversation to a safer subject than where he happened to be. Suddenly his father sounded tired and defeated. It was a moment of worry for Cory.

"I'm fine, Cory. I guess it's just a part of being a parent that we wonder how we let our work keep us from our kids. Don't worry. I'm fine. Are you eating well and enjoying your summer?" Without waiting for an answer, he continued. "I'm sorry, son, but the job here might drag out another two weeks beyond the month I had expected. I wish I could be home with you, but I simply can't," his father explained.

"That's okay, Dad," Cory replied, hoping he didn't sound too eager. "We'll have plenty of time this fall."

"Have you thought more about playing football as a senior, Cory?" his father questioned, hesitantly.

After a few moments of silence, Cory gave his father what he wanted to hear. "Yes, Dad, I'm thinking about it."

"That's good, son. We'll talk more about it when I return."

The cell phone snapped shut and Cory felt a moment of relief. While successfully evading the questions, he hadn't outwardly lied to his father and, although he would someday pay for his deception, he desperately needed to spend this summer where no one could badger him about football every hour of the day. If he played the game, it had to be by HIS choice.

On one of the most beautiful days of June, three weeks after he had arrived, Cory finished a huge breakfast of wild strawberries, thick oatmeal, and boiled crayfish, grabbed his compass and pedometer, and headed toward the south. Wearing old tennis shoes and cut off jeans, he waded boldly through the creek and into the swampy reeds on the other side. Somewhere in this direction, he was sure from his vague memory, there was more water to be found. A blurred picture of his mother and father in a boat with him as a small child floated in his mind. Since he had never gone any farther than the creek, south of it was the most logical place to explore.

On the other side of the creek, the area had larger, taller pines with a carpet of pine needles covering the forest floor. Walking was easier here and after picking the ticks from his legs, Cory struck out in a more rapid pace, carrying the .22 rifle.

Almost every day he spent a few minutes shooting at his leaf targets, now dried and curled and much harder to hit on the side of the shed. But practice was, indeed, paying off. Some of his leaf targets had been hit so often that they were reduced to small specks just large enough to be seen. The shotgun, on the other hand, proved to be super easy when he blasted old glass bottles that he'd found half buried in a garbage pile at the edge of the woods. Set in a row on the top of a large tree stump while he stood a mere twenty feet away, the targets were extremely simple to smash. However, when Cory rigged a small sapling into a catapult that sent the bottles flying through the air, the game suddenly became a real challenge. Every practice was intense. He needed to learn and become good at it without using too much of his ammunition. Each shotgun shell and each bullet for the rifle might mean food or safety.

Like every sport Cory had conquered in the past, this

too appeared to be easily learned. Already he could hit three out of four of his "flying ducks." What bothered him the most was the fact that no hunting season was open during the summer, and any killing of animals would be illegal. Therefore, he would hunt only as a last resort.

Carrying the rifle now was a matter of safety and would be used solely for protection. Cory shifted it to his other arm and checked the pedometer. Diligently watching his compass, he had kept true south and estimated his distance at two miles. Climbing a small hill, he paused at the crest. There below him lay what he was hoping to find. A tiny lake, probably no larger than five acres, rested calmly within a circle of trees. When he reached the water's edge, he noted that the shore was reedy and irregular except for where he stood. Here gravel and sand covered a small area where someone had labored to place them. Extending out only a few feet into the lake, the sand suddenly dropped away. With water as clear as glass, Cory thought the tiny lake must be spring fed. This is the water he remembered.

Memories of his mother came to him in pieces as he stood there—good memories, although vague and limited. It pained him to have forgotten so much after the shock of her death, but from time to time small fragments surfaced in his mind like benchmarks through the fog. Now, was one of those times and he sat down on the sand to enjoy his thoughts. They had had a picnic here and while he remembered sitting on a blanket in this very spot when he was perhaps three or four years old, he couldn't form a clear picture of his mother now. People often referred to her as having been lovely. But what did that mean and why was he unable to remember her face?

Making a snap decision, Cory shook off his shoes and dove into the lake for a refreshing swim. It depressed him to think of his mother and not recall what she looked like.

As he stroked to the other side and back, he let the memories that refused to form, slip away and concentrated on the beauty of the lake. Not only would the vigorous swim suffice as a bath, but the biting cold of the water refreshed his senses and he headed back to the cabin, planning the dock he intended to build for the lake—HIS lake!

The moment Cory stepped into the clearing that surrounded the cabin, he knew something wasn't the same. With his senses alert, he moved slowly toward the cabin, letting his eyes sweep the yard and buildings for any changes. Was that were he had left the rake this morning and was the rocker in the same spot? He shifted the rifle to his right hand and with the feeling that he was being watched, he quietly ascended the porch steps and approached the door. In one quick movement he slammed it open. The cabin was empty!

On the table, however, was a wonderful sight. Along with a jar of jam, a large stick of sausage, three real apples, two oranges, and a loaf of what looked like homemade bread, was a quart of milk. Immediately chugging down half the milk, Cory thought of Annie. That was the only possible explanation and he knew he would have to see her again.

Since his arrival, Cory was aware that he had lost some of his weight. His six-foot-two-inch frame was considered to be quite lean, although muscular, and someone was always suggesting that he "bulk up". But no matter how much he consumed now, a diet of wild greens, fruit, and fish would not add any extra pounds this summer. For the moment, however, he had a feast fit for a king and he would enjoy every little bite.

As each warm day faded into a variety of beautiful sunsets, Cory's time at the cabin evolved into a comfortable routine. With morning came the fetching of water, the capture of fish for the day and the gathering of fresh greens—dandelion, cress, plantain, purslane (or *Portulaca oleracea* as Mr. Bellington, his biology teacher, would say). Afternoons were for cutting more lawn to reduce the tick menace since they were more prevalent in the tall grass, and then time was given to exploring the forest. Evenings meant music and reading in his favorite spot—the rocker on the porch. And, of course, before sleep he needed to remove the wood ticks that wanted so desperately to use his body as a blood bank.

Although cutting back the branches that hung over the paths that he walked each day and keeping the grass cut short greatly diminished his encounter with the inevitable ticks, one particular evening brought Cory some concern when he discovered that a tick had attached itself to the very center of his back and repeated efforts to remove it were futile. With his fingers stretched out and his arm twisted as far as possible, he could just touch the edge of the tick. But to grab it and pull it out was hopeless. Cory couldn't leave it. Once attached, the ticks would feed off the blood of their host, gorging themselves and swelling to more than twenty times their original size. Since they often transmitted diseases to their victims, it was wise to remove them. Now, HE needed Annie.

Confused by his first reaction to her and yet wanting to thank her for the food she had left on his table, he had hesitated to look for her in case she would misinterpret his thanks as a plea for more. But now he needed someone to remove the tick and she was the only one to whom he could turn.

With three freshly caught fish for a gift, Cory left the cabin very early the next morning to find Annie. The day promised to be a hot one with steadily rising humidity and he wanted to be back in time to haul the parts of his premade dock to the lake in the afternoon and still get home by early evening. Twice on the long trek he needed to retrace his steps before he found the spot where he had first seen her. Placing himself where he thought he had been standing and visualizing her pointing in the direction of her home, he continued through the woods on that route.

In only a few minutes, Cory was assured that he was heading the right way. Someone was cooking and the sweet smell wafted through the humid air. Coming upon a path, he followed it into a clearing in time to see Annie remove something from an outdoor oven and carry it to her porch, a huge black dog jumping at her side.

While slightly larger, her log cabin was a perfect copy of his, right down to the porch and the handmade furniture on it. He stopped to watch her and although she had her back to him, she spoke.

"Welcome to my home, Cory," she said as she turned to face him, restraining the dog with her fingers under his collar.

"Hi," he responded, suddenly feeling foolish and wondering why she wasn't surprised to see him.

"This is Brute," she explained, indicating the dog as she released him and, in commands, brought him over to meet Cory. The name fit the dog who nuzzled and carefully smelled him for future recognition.

"You're just in time for chocolate cake," she invited.

"I brought you some fish to say thank you for the food you left on my table," he explained, handing her the wrapped fish.

The slight widening of her intensely blue eyes and the soft smile on her lips told him that she was pleased. "Ah," she said, "my favorite food!"

"Come, sit. I'll get us something to drink. Would you like milk or coffee? Soda?" she asked with one hand holding the door open. When he didn't respond and he hadn't moved, she let the screen door slam shut. "What's wrong, Cory?"

"I…I need some help," he blurted. "It's not really all that important, but I can't do it myself." Now, he felt childish and silly. "It's a tick," he explained. "It's imbedded in my back and I can't reach it."

Expecting laughter, Cory was surprised instead when she pulled a Leatherman tool from her pocket and ordered him to turn around and remove his shirt. It took only seconds for her to pull out the tick and swab the area with alcohol. "Promise me you will never ignore a tick that is imbedded," she demanded. Looking at him intently, she waited for an answer.

Following his absolute promise, they sat on the porch consuming her chocolate cake. While she had coffee, he gratefully drank two large glasses of milk with enough warm cake smothered in chocolate sauce to compensate for all the desserts he had missed in his entire life.

"Cory, I assume you are staying in your cabin alone?" Annie inquired when they had finished. "Your parents aren't with you?"

"My mother died about twelve years ago and my dad is in India for a month, but it's just fine with my dad that I am here," he answered rapidly. "He owns about eighty acres with the small cabin and he calls to check on me every other evening." In perhaps a too-hurried tone, Cory rushed on to explain further. "Except for this tick thing, I have been doing great. I have a garden planted and I get fish and other food. Plus I have a supply of dried foods if I need them. You're alone, too, aren't you, Annie? Or do you have family with you here?"

She smiled. The light was behind her and it illuminated the stray hairs that escaped her braid, framing her face with a halo of white. She knew he was being deceptive. And he could tell by her smile, that she knew.

"Yes, I'm alone too. My parents aren't with me either," she said.

Now she was teasing him, but he went on. "No children, no husband?" he questioned.

A flash of pain crossed her face and she shook her head before answering. "I had a wonderful husband and two beautiful children." She paused. "They're dead."

The words came out with a struggle and Cory was immediately sorry he had asked. He liked Annie and wanted to cause her no pain. "I'm sorry," he apologized.

It was time to go. He had opened a wound and he could see she needed time to be alone. Thanking her again for the food and the new provisions that she stacked in his arms, he struck out for home.

By dark that evening, he had carried all the pre-made sections of his dock to the lake and staked out the exact position in which it would be placed the next day. After a refreshing bath in the lake, Cory returned to a very hot cabin, a quick meal, and a good night's sleep on the front porch without so much as one note from his guitar.

The next morning, as he trudged through the woods with a pack of tools and some food for lunch, his mind was enthusiastically occupied with his construction plans. The dock would be rather small and anchored only on one end because of the sudden drop and depth of the lake, but it would be just fine for his simple needs. Estimating that it would take most of the day, he increased his pace. At the top of the hill, before descending to the lake, Cory came to an abrupt halt. Where he had placed the pieces of his unassembled dock, there was nothing! Even the stakes that marked the dock's position had been pulled out of the ground and taken. Rapidly descending the hill, Cory's eyes searched the area for some clue. After the initial shock, and convincing himself that his eyes weren't betraying him, he shifted his gaze to the rest of the lake, unconsciously expecting to see the pieces being carried away by a thief. There on the shore, directly opposite where he stood, was a strange, but familiar feature. Staring straight at him was a brand new dock, exactly like the one he had planned!

Chapter 3

Totally confused by what he thought he was seeing, Cory stood there and stared at the dock. From this distance he couldn't be sure it was his. But how could anyone have carried his dock from here to there, assembled it, and anchored it in the ground in so little time, unless they worked through the night? If that dock was his, he intended to take it back.

Striking out for the other side of the lake, Cory soon learned that the irregular shore was, in fact, a reed-filled swamp on both the west and the east side, where excess water from the lake overflowed its banks. By the time he had gone back into the woods to circumvent the swamp and struggled through the debris of fallen trees and thick brush that lined the rest of the shore, his anger was no longer under control.

When he finally reached the dock, it took only a moment to recognize his own work—small saw marks where he had misjudged the length of a pole or chunks of bark that he had not completely removed from a log. Incredibly, this was HIS dock! Angrily he dropped his sack of tools and grabbing his crowbar, he tackled the dismantling with all the anger he felt inside. Leaving the entire top in one piece, Cory strapped the sack of tools to his body and with all the stength he could gather, he started dragging part of his dock back to HIS side of the lake, through the woods and around the swamp.

Exhausted but still as angry, Cory dropped that piece of the dock where he had originally planned to place it and returned to the other side of the lake for the rest of the sections. He wasn't sure how deep the posts had been sunk and wondered if he would be able to remove them.

By putting all his weight against one of them and pushing it back and forth in the sand, the post slowly could be pulled from the ground. Just as he set it down, a voice startled him.

"Hey!" it shouted angrily. "What are you doing?"

Cory looked up to see an angry young girl about his own age clad in a bright green bathing suit standing a short distance away with her hands on her hips and a towel draped over her shoulder. Slowly he stood up, keeping his eyes locked on hers. As mad, tired, and sweaty as he was at the moment, his patience with a demanding thief was gone.

In a commanding voice, she repeated the question. "What are you doing? Who do you think you are that you have the right to steal MY dock?" she shouted.

Cory could take no more. As he struggled to carefully control his voice, he attempted to clarify things to this very pretty but obviously demented person. "This," he said, pointing to the remains of his dock, "happens to be MINE—the same dock I carried with a great deal of effort all the way from MY cabin to this lake last evening on THAT side of the shore with the intention of installing it this morning. But to my surprise," he continued sarcastically, "a thief stole it during…"

"Thief!" she screamed. "YOU are calling ME a thief when I catch you in the act of taking MY dock?"

Since reasoning with her was going to be like reasoning with an ant, Cory threw up his hands in frustration and resumed the task of getting the support poles out of the ground. Glancing up at her angry face while he began leaning his weight against the second piling, he saw her place two fingers into her mouth and to his surprise, made an incredibly loud, piercing whistle. Ignoring her, he continued pushing and pulling the post, jerking it back and forth as he moved in a circle until it was loose enough to pull out. As he lowered the cedar post to the ground where the first one lay, he glanced up to see trouble.

Just a few feet in front and to the side of the young girl was a very big fellow, maybe a few years older than Cory, a few inches taller, and twice as wide. Here was the typical football player, and at the moment he, too, looked angry. In a growl, he said, "The dock stays!"

Even the tiniest remnant of patience was no longer available to Cory and with calm resignation he left the edge of the water and walked directly up to his "problem".

"Let me introduce my brother, Gobb," the girl said with a smirk. "Maybe now you'll realize that the dock stays HERE!"

Reasoning was clearly not going to work with either of them and Cory was now too angry to let go of the situation. He delivered the blow swiftly and deliberately aimed at Gobb's face with all the power and speed he could produce, sending him reeling backward. However, before he could hit the ground, two more fellows, slightly closer to Cory's weight, stepped into the clearing. "I'd like you to meet two more of my brother's, Coonsey and Truck," the girl stated defiantly, then stepped aside, knowing they would settle the issue.

Although Cory returned quite a few of the blows that he received, the final humiliation came when he was lofted into the lake by the three overpowering morons. Since there was absolutely no point in continuing a fight he could not possibly win, Cory treaded water to remove his tennis shoes and tie them to his belt loops. Then, taking one last angry look at the four standing by the posts of his dock, he wiped the blood from his face with the back of his hand and turned slowly to swim across the lake. He would make new posts and would have to be satisfied with the fact that he had at least recovered the entire top of his dock, which, when he reached the shore, he padlocked to a tree for the night.

When he returned the next morning, dragging four new cedar posts for the dock, he thought of the young girl he met yesterday. The lake was on his dad's property and obviously she thought she had a right to swim there, but why would they think they had a right to build a dock there? He had to admit that she was really a very pretty brunette with a great shape, but an awful disposition! She had been almost as angry as he was.

By three o'clock the dock was finished and Cory stepped back to survey his efforts. Although not sturdy enough to hold many people, there was enough space to lie in the sun after a swim and with that thought he plunged into the lake to check it out. At the end of the dock, Cory had attached a small rope ladder and after climbing up, he stretched out on the log top.

For days he had worn only shorts and tennis shoes, making it easier to remove the ticks and enjoy the sunshine. It was all part of the freedom he felt and other than the incident yesterday, his summer was progressing very nicely. He had rarely been forced to think of football even though he knew it was a necessary topic that required a lot of thought and a final decision. This was the end of the first month at the cabin and the decision about football was no closer to being settled in Cory's mind. Why were guys, who were big enough and strong enough like yesterday's three linebackers, heroes only because they played football? It didn't make sense!

Cory spent that evening at the lake, alternately swimming and quietly playing his guitar. Several deer, a raccoon, and numerous birds came for a drink while he played, apparently undisturbed by the gentle music.

Although it was nearly nine o'clock when the sun finally set, he stayed to watch the clouds in the sky shift from golden orange to pink and purple, before he returned to the cabin.

Two days after the fight at the lake, while Cory knelt on the lawn attempting to sharpen the blades of the lawn mower, he saw a flash of color moving through the trees beyond the creek. He sat back to watch and could hardly believe his eyes. Coming up the path was the girl from the lake. She was dressed in cut-off jeans and a bright red tank top. Her thick brown hair hung down to her shoulders rather than pulled back from her face as it had been at the lake. She walked with a sense of confidence and purpose.

Cory never cared much for girls who were bold, demanding, and bossy. They were usually unkind, unthinking, and selfish. The traits all seemed to go together.

Once she reached the lawn, she stopped.

Cory had risen and, since he had nothing nice to say to her, he simply placed his hands on his hips and stared at her.

For a moment she seemed to hesitate—perhaps not as sure of herself as she wanted others to think? Then, she spoke.

"The dock was my birthday present from my brothers," she began, "and I came to get reimbursement since it's now in YOUR possession."

Cory smiled and shook his head in disbelief. "Do you usually receive stolen property as gifts for your birthday?" he asked.

"YOU are the thief," she shouted, "and YOU know it!"

With that outburst, Cory had had enough! "Look,"

he commanded, gritting his teeth and grabbing her arm as he pulled her over to the path. "See that stump?" he said, pointing to it. "That's the first tree I cut for the dock!" Dragging her roughly he pointed to another. "That's another! And there! And there!" Still pulling her along, he showed her the pile of sawdust and peels of bark where he had assembled some of the pieces.

As he let go of her, he suddenly felt ashamed that he had been so rough. "I'm sorry," he said, "I didn't mean to hurt you, but the truth is that I made the dock no matter what your brothers tell you."

Confusion was written all over her face as she backed away from him, then turned and ran down the path without saying another word. Cory couldn't tell whether she had believed him or not, but he was certain that the problem with the dock was not over.

A much more important decision weighed heavily on Cory's mind all week as he went about his normal routine. It was July already and in less than two weeks his father would be home from India. The last thing Cory wanted was to frighten his dad by letting him arrive home to find his son gone. As much as Cory needed to be alone this summer, he could not cause his dad more stress by either lying or letting him think that his son had run away. Each explanation that he devised in his head was immediately tossed aside as too deceitful, too improbable, or too unkind. Then, of course, there was always the truth.

Cory's food supply was getting better; his garden was beginning to produce, he found more wild things to consume along with his fish, and he had received another feast of bread, cheese, and some milk from Annie. Raspberries would soon be ripe and following that, the blackberries would be in season.

But on Saturday of that week, he faced a new problem. He was terribly sick. When he woke in the morning, he had pains in his stomach and by noon, he had crawled into bed with a raging fever. Slowly the afternoon, evening, and night passed in terrifying dreams, or wakeful restlessness. By the next day, Cory was too weak to get out of bed and found he was sweating profusely. An incredible thirst plagued him while he lay on the bed in the loft but he simply could not get to the kitchen for water. He spent an exhausting morning slipping back into bouts of sleep and wild dreams.

Then, somewhere, lost in the middle of his dreams, a distant voice called his name. While his senses struggled toward consciousness, the voice grew louder.

"Cory? Are you here?"

Cory opened his eyes and tried to sit up but couldn't. He was sure he was awake when he heard his name again and suddenly he realized that someone was in the cabin.

"Annie?" he groaned.

"Cory, where are you? What's the matter?"

It took every ounce of effort to answer. "I'm in the loft. I'm sick," he said.

While he lay there in agony, he heard the sound of Annie in the kitchen pouring water from his kettle on the stove and then, in moments, she was up the ladder and helping him. Cool, wonderful water poured slowly down his parched throat as he relaxed against the brace of pillows she had stacked under him. Cory never knew that water could taste so good.

"What happened?" she asked, as she carefully washed his face with a cool, wet cloth, pushing his thick blond hair aside.

"I don't know. All of a sudden I was sick."

It stunned Cory when she placed her lips on his forehead and as Annie pulled away, she explained with a smile. "That's what mothers do. You still have a slight fever but I suspect that the worst is over."

"Thanks," he mumbled, feeling foolish but already so much better.

"Cory, what have you been eating?"

After a full explanation of the wild plants and berries that he had been gathering, Annie pointed out that several of them were safe to eat only in the spring and became dangerous when consumed too late in the summer. Making a mental note of this new information, Cory vowed to avoid the plants he now knew were the cause of his illness.

Once Cory had downed enough water to quench his thirst and to begin the process of rehydrating his body, Annie brought him a small jar of milk and a piece of fresh-baked bread from the supplies she had left on the table below. While she sat on the side of the bed watching him eat, he, in turn, watched her. Those incredible blue eyes of hers said more than when she spoke. They told him when she was pleased and when she was lonely, like now.

"Annie, how do you get supplies to your cabin?" he asked between bites, thinking of the flour that she would need in order to make his slice of bread.

"Actually, I cheat!" she confessed laughingly. "You've not been at my place long enough to see the other side of my cabin where I park a four-wheeler. Nor would you know that I have only a four-mile trip on it to reach my Jeep. From there I have about six miles of sand road to a blacktop one and then only about twenty-five miles to the store in Woodville. During the winter I have a snowmobile to get me to my Jeep and since the area off the sand road is still being logged, they keep it fairly well-plowed." Her laughter was full and rich.

Cory stared in awe and disbelief. "You live here all year? By yourself?" he stammered.

She nodded with a broad smile.

"In winter?"

She nodded again.

Cory was speechless. How could she manage living here all alone through the long winter even with transportation? "You have electricity," he stated as a matter of fact.

"Yes, and a backup generator, so I'm quite comfortable. But let's talk about you, Cory. When was the last time you had a huge hamburger on the grill?"

Annie was full of surprises and her laughter told him that she enjoyed his reaction. The thought of a juicy hamburger was extremely pleasant and he realized that he was getting well. Finally he admitted that it was a long time since he had tasted one, which prompted an invitation to join her for an outdoor picnic next Tuesday, giving him a few days to fully recover from his sickness.

The day of the big picnic came with perfect weather—a clear, sunny sky, and eighty-three, dry degrees. Since every trip to Annie's was an education in getting through the thick brush, fallen trees in the woods, the muck of the swamps, and around the brambles of the berry patches, Cory modified it each time to a shorter and clearer path. Now he traversed it in the record time of two hours—half the time it took on the first trip. In rhythm with the weather, he wore cut-off jeans and tennis shoes with a tee shirt tied to his belt loop. Slow steady exposure to the sun over the past six weeks had given his body a deep tan, and the freedom he felt with fewer clothes intensified his sense of well-being. In the small clearings that occurred between sections of the forest, he gathered wild flowers with the intention of presenting his bouquet to Annie along with two small fish he had caught before starting out this morning.

As soon as he came within sight of her cabin, he could smell homemade bread and something sweet like cookies or cake. He quickened his pace and seeing no one outside he went to the screen door and knocked. Only, it wasn't Annie who came to the door. It was the girl from the lake. Instinctively, Cory backed away from the door.

"Hi," she said almost shyly.

Was this the same girl? The brunette hair was swept away from her face and clipped high on the back of her head. Wisps of slightly curly strands hung loosely around her neck and face, giving her a sweet, innocent look. Shorts and tank top with sandals agreed with the day. But she was smiling and it transformed her face from angry, as he had seen it before, into beautiful. Was this the same girl? They stared at each other. Then Cory turned to leave, wondering if this was some kind of cruel joke or a set-up.

Before he had a chance to descend the steps, Annie came around the corner from the back of the cabin carrying an axe.

"Hi," she greeted him. "I see you've met Jenny. I hope you introduced yourselves," she said with the clear assumption that they had.

"Sorry, we haven't," he said bluntly. "Here are some flowers for you, Annie, and a couple of fish," he explained, handing them to her. "I can't stay. I have other things I need to do this afternoon."

"Cory!" was all Annie said, as he started to walk away, but her tone held a note of disappointment and confusion.

He turned and looked into the incredible blue eyes, wanting to explain his poor behavior when the screen door slammed and Jenny came down the steps.

"It's me, Annie. I'm the problem here." She looked directly at Cory. "I don't even know your name and yet we have this big argument between us."

"Look, if you expect Annie to get me to pay you for the dock you…"

"NO! No," she protested quickly. "I want to apologize to you. After you showed me where you had sawed the logs and worked on the dock, I confronted my brothers. They finally had to admit the truth when they couldn't even agree on where they had gotten the materials."

While she spoke, Cory couldn't help noticing the remains of a large bruise on her left arm where he had angrily grabbed her. Shame engulfed him. "I think the apology should be mine," he admitted.

Aware that he had noticed the bruise, she started laughing. "You mean this?" she asked, pointing to it. "This is nothing! I have five older brothers. You can't even begin to imagine the bruises I've gotten from them!"

"I think a hand shake is called for at this time," Annie said with a grin, "and then we have an old-fashioned picnic to attend."

Fitting the occasion, Annie offered them cold potato salad, fresh fruit salad, chips, grilled hamburgers or cheeseburgers, lemonade or soda, and a platter of just-baked chocolate chip cookies. Knowing that he would not have this kind of food for some time, Cory lingered over every bite while they chatted about the names of Jenny's brothers.

Early in life each of Jenny's five brothers had acquired a nickname fitting a particular incident or obsession. Greg, the oldest, was named "Coonsey" because he had had a pet raccoon when he was just four and it would respond only to him. Nick, the biggest, was not only built like a "Truck" even when young, but now he was always working on one. Matt was named "Gobb" for a foolish reason that Cory could only guess and Jenny would not reveal in order to protect her personal safety. Tom was called "Chunk" and it had nothing to do with his tall and hefty size. He loved chunky peanut butter to the extent that it had to be locked away when brought home from the store. Finally, Alex, Cory's age, the youngest and the smallest of the boys by their standards, was "Pooter," a name derived from his favorite vocabulary word from the day he first spoke. "Poo."

The afternoon was gone too quickly and as Cory trudged through the woods to his cabin he realized that he still knew very little about Annie, although she did give him a tour of her property. Then too, all he had learned about Jenny was that she lived with her parents and five brothers about six miles south of Cory. The fact that they all lived in the area the whole year surprised him. Unlike him, however, they had the extremely important modern conveniences of plumbing and electricity, which would certainly make a difference.

Living with five brothers, three of whom he had the misfortune of meeting at the lake when they disagreed over the ownership of the dock, must be unpleasant. He could picture them giving Jenny a hard time about everything. Although he still did not trust her, she was slowly redeeming herself in his eyes. After all, she had been polite and helpful to Annie, and she DID apologize to him. Still...there was something about Jenny that made him unsure of her.

Chapter 4

Several weeks ago, Cory had explored the area of the woods to the northwest of his cabin. A few small fields in that direction held thick patches of raspberry bushes bursting with unripe green berries. This year the weather had been most cooperative with rain and warm sunshine at just the right times, promising a huge crop of berries. If Cory's calculations were correct, the raspberries should now be ripening.

On Thursday, as soon as the dew evaporated from the grass, he set out to harvest the berries. Dressed in hiking boots, long jeans, a long-sleeved shirt to protect himself from the thorns on the brambles, and carrying two medium-sized pails, he started out for the biggest patch about two miles from the cabin.

The day was beautiful! A few fluffy, white clouds floated in the deep blue sky while Cory wound his way through the trees to the field he had scouted more than two weeks ago. While he walked, he reviewed again the problem that he had come to the cabin to resolve. Once more he selected and discarded the pros and cons of playing football his senior year to please his dad and earn a scholarship, versus continuing his musical studies and struggling on his own. Wasn't the fact that he was living on his own this summer, proof that he could make it without anyone's help? Then, he thought of Annie. Technically, he wasn't living on his own. How many times had she helped him? Would he have made it without her? Doubts assailed him.

The second problem that plagued him, he would encounter in just one week. What could he tell his dad before he arrived home from India and found Cory gone?

How could he explain his absence? With a lie? Or with the truth.

Cory was so deep in thought that he nearly missed the field, having to retrace his steps twice. But it was worth the effort. The patch was more than he expected. The healthy-looking raspberry bushes were laden with huge, juicy globes of red fruit, larger than any wild berries he had ever seen.

Strapping the handle of the pail to his belt, Cory began eagerly picking the fruit, sampling as he worked. Leaving the unripe and too ripe berries, he slowly moved from one side of the patch to the other. Several times he went down on his haunches to retrieve the biggest of the berries hidden among the thick covering of green leaves.

It was during this time, while crouching between the tall plants that Cory heard a movement among the brambles of the raspberries on the west side of the patch. Slowly he stood up. Not more than thirty feet directly in front of him was the curved back of an exceptionally large black bear pulling berries roughly from their stems with his tongue.

Cory froze as the bear rose on his hind legs to a surprising height, suddenly aware of a human sharing his food. With arms at his sides, the pail of raspberries hanging from one hand and not a muscle moving, Cory watched the bear while the bear stared at him.

Then movement and a whiney sound to the left of where Cory stood clarified his dilemma. The bear was not a HE; it was a SHE! And her cub was eating berries about ten feet from Cory.

A low warning grunt issued from the mother as she remained upright surveying the threat to her cub. Then she lowered her massive body and with eyes locked on Cory, she plowed slowly through the patch heading directly to him.

"Don't run! Don't run!" screamed in Cory's head. He had heard that advice repeatedly over the years. Bears can easily outrun a human. They also climb trees with speed and ease. There is no place to run, so don't!

While maintaining an immobile stance with incredible effort, Cory could now smell the strong odor of the bear advancing toward him only a few feet away.

Another warning growl drifted his way.

A soft breeze shifted his hair and he hoped the movement would mean nothing to the bear. When the bear's nose touched his shirt and snifted his clothing, it took every ounce of Cory's self-discipline to remain still, but he had absolutely no control over the involuntary shudder that swept over him as the bear licked his right hand. Moving around him, she found the pail of raspberries and placing her snout into the bucket, pulled it from Cory's hand, dropping it to the ground with a sharp rattle. With a jerk, she pulled her head away, sniffed loudly, then slowly returned to gobble the berries.

Out of the corner of his eye Cory had been simultaneously watching both bears, noting that the cub was slowly getting farther and farther away from him. Now, as the mother licked up the last of the berries, she raised her head to Cory's left hand, brushed it with her rough tongue, then turned, and slowly plodded after her cub. When they were no longer in sight, Cory let out a loud moan and sat down on the overturned pail, burying his face in his hands.

He thought of the guns back in the cabin that he had carried everywhere those first weeks, then abandoned when he realized that he could not bring himself to kill an animal. He knew he had been lucky this time. Next time… He shuddered! As he sat there a few moments, irritation set in. Those raspberries were for his dinner and he had as much right to them as the bears. With new energy he returned to the process of harvesting them, choosing to place them, however, only in the pail that had none of the bear's slobber.

The incident with the mother bear and her cub was not one to be forgotten easily, and it reinforced the practical side of carrying a weapon. Despite his reluctance to shoot an animal, Cory knew that if a human life was in danger, he would do whatever was necessary. There are moments in life that bring together all the ingredients to form a new perspective and as Cory trekked home with his hard-won raspberries, he made some important decisions.

First, he would start carrying either a large hunting knife or a gun at all times and second, he would be honest with his father when the time came to explain where he was and why. For now, the raspberries were on his mind and he was wishing he had milk to pour over them, when upon arrival home, he found that Annie had left a few more provisions, including a pint of milk.

That evening as Cory sat on the porch in the rocker practicing the notes of one of his favorite songs, the phone rang. The call from his father was right on time. Bracing himself for an uncomfortable conversation, Cory opened his cell phone. "Hi, Dad," he said.

"How did you know it was me?" his dad asked. "Don't you ever get calls from any of your friends?"

"Well, not often," Cory answered, hesitantly but truthfully. "I haven't spent a lot of time with friends this summer. I needed time to think about things…like football…and music."

When Cory stopped talking, there was a long pause of silence. Then with a suspicious note in his voice his father asked, "Where are you, Cory?"

"Well… I had this chance to spend some time camping up north," Cory began. "Do you remember how much fun it used to be when we went to the cabin, Dad?"

In silence he waited for an answer to his question, but instead, his father only repeated his own question. "Where are you, Cory?" This time there was a demanding tone in his voice.

"I'm at our cabin in the national forest, Dad."

The silence that greeted Cory was unbearable. Would his father be that angry that he could not speak? Or was Cory's presence at the cabin an unforgivable act? In reality, he had never disobeyed his father. Actually, there had never been a rule that he was NOT to go to the cabin. He waited.

"I take it you're planning to stay there for the summer?" his father finally asked.

"I'm hoping you'll let me," Cory replied, clearly indicating that he knew the decision was his dad's.

There was more silence while the question hung in the air. His father was known for never making foolish, snap decisions. That was one of his strengths in the world of international business and often measured the importance of the decision. At the moment, the outcome was important to both of them.

" Stay where you are Cory and be safe," his father finally said. " I'll join you as soon as I can in about a week. That is, if you don't object," he added.

"That sounds just fine with me," Cory admitted with a grin.

After a moment of silence, his dad added, " I love you, Cory!"

"I love you too, Dad."

The grin stayed on Cory's face for several minutes after he closed his phone. Letting go of their recent arguments, he resumed plucking the strings of the guitar, while trying to remember the rare occasions when he had spent some time with his father. Sadly, only events that involved sports came to mind. Together here at the cabin, he hoped it would be different.

With one of the problems worrying Cory now settled, he spent the next two days tackling the special projects that he had been designing in his head for weeks. Each morning he walked to the creek and carried two large buckets of water back to the cabin, and if his garden needed water or he wanted to bathe or wash clothes, he made several more tedious trips to the creek and back. It was time to change this routine.

What Cory lacked in construction skills, he made up with intelligence. He had already made a small paddlewheel which, when placed in the creek, would scoop up the water as the current forced it to turn. Each scoop of water would be dumped into a trough as every circle was completed. A series of logs, split down the center and hollowed out, would be placed end to end all the way to the cabin. Ingenious as it was, Cory constructed three different wheels before he had one the right size to compensate for the slowness of the stream and the elevation of the ground around the cabin. Granted, the flow of water would not be tremendous, but a steady stream would still fill the large copper tub that he found in the shed.

To complete his project, Cory needed a number of eight-inch-diameter logs to make into troughs. He had already removed several trees for his dock from the area around the cabin and those that remained were needed for shade and could not be sacrificed for the project. If his memory was correct, the perfect size for the troughs would be found to the southeast of the lake.

Choosing a warm and sunny morning, Cory packed an axe, saw, and a few other tools along with rope into a sack, attached the large hunting knife that he wore constantly strapped to his belt and started out to get his logs. Fully aware that this project would take extra time and a great deal of energy to drag the logs back to the cabin, he brought food and water for the day.

The hike to the southeast side of the lake was more difficult as the spring growth had thickened to full summer status and areas of impassable brush had to be avoided. Nearly two miles from the cabin, Cory began to hear the distant sounds of a chain saw coming from the direction he was headed. His dad would never have contracted to have the land logged off. The property held too many painful memories and, as much as Cory knew, was never even thought of, much less dealt with on a business level. So who was cutting down trees?

Moving as quickly as possible he headed directly toward the sound. There was more than one chain saw, but it was difficult to guess how many men might be involved. Entering an area of tall, thin pines between stands of hardwood trees, Cory could make out the flash of movement among the trees in the distance. As he neared the area, the loggers took on a familiar appearance and, by the time he reached them, it was clear. In the momentary silence between the chain saw action, Cory dropped his bag of tools with a clang, announcing his arrival to Jenny's brothers.

"Wait! Don't tell me," Cory spit out sarcastically. "That must be 'Truck' over there and you must be 'Chunk'," he said, facing the fellow closest to him. "Thought maybe I should let you know that, as usual, the stuff you're taking, doesn't belong to you."

None of them seemed surprised to see him and in the different positions of their work, each one had merely stopped what they were doing. Piles of wood, split and stacked on a small skid indicated that they had been at this for some time already.

"I'll give you credit for one thing 'Bigshot', Gobb replied with his hands on his hips and sweat running off his brow. "You are either incredibly brave, or stupid." With that, he dropped the axe he was holding and walked over to Cory.

Although he remained nonchalantly leaning against the tree with his sack of tools at his feet, Cory knew what was coming and prepared himself mentally and physically for a fight, praying that Gobb's signal to his brothers really meant that the fight was just between the two of them.

Speed and agility were on Cory's side, but the strength of each blow from Gobb's larger size took its toll. It was clear, finally, that both of them had had enough. Each of them had a bloody nose and bruises were beginning to form on their faces when the fighting suddenly stopped with an undeclared winner. Winded and staring at each other, an unspoken declaration of respect seemed to pass between them and then it suddenly vaporized.

"Get off our land," Gobb commanded.

"We'll see whose land it is," replied Cory calmly as they each turned and walked away. He picked up his tools and moved into the pines, wiping the blood from his nose with his shirt. At the edge of the pines he set the tools down. He intended to finish the job he had come to do. Looking back, he saw the last of the brothers pulling the skid filled with firewood and he couldn't help wondering what kind of football players they were. From Jenny, he knew that Alex or "Pooter" was Cory's age, "Truck" had just graduated and the other three were in college. They were the most aggravating guys he had ever met.

Gobb's demand that Cory was on their land, had stolen some of his anger when the fight began. What if he was right? What if this really was their land? Then he would be as guilty of stealing as they were. He would have to find the truth.

After a few moments of hesitation, Cory cut down one of the pines, cleared it of branches and began hauling it toward home. If he really was on their land, he would pay them for the tree. For now, he had a trough to build.

Chapter 5

It was a matter of pride that sent Cory off to find Annie the next morning. He needed to clarify the boundaries of his father's property to satisfy his fear that he might be guilty of trespassing and stealing. Things like honesty, courage, kindness, and perseverance were the traits that made a boy into a man in Cory's mind, not football as his dad seemed to think. Strangely these were the very values his father stressed, both in his own actions and in his speech, and yet football always clouded the issue. Now, if Cory was wrong, a correction needed to be made and the next time he encountered Jenny's brothers, he wanted to be sure of his own position.

Before leaving the cabin, Cory placed his two freshly caught fish into a small pail and pulled three of his biggest carrots, though still rather small, from the garden. He never went to Annie's without a simple expression of his appreciation for all she did for him.

On each trip, Cory redesigned the path he took through the stretches of forest and clearings, even cutting growth from time to time in order to make the journey to Annie's faster and easier. If he kept a steady pace, the trip could now be made in less than two hours instead of the five hours it had taken him the first time. Knowing that he would be traveling through a few berry patches, Cory picked up the shotgun and a few shells as he closed the cabin door.

When he reached the halfway point on the trail to Annie's, he checked the sky once more and knew that the weather was changing. White clouds had given way to gray ones and the wind was noticeably stronger. He was already aware of the dropping temperature. A storm was coming.

Just as the first crack of thunder hit, Cory broke into the clearing around Annie's cabin. She was struggling to pull a large crock off the porch. He hurried to help her put it into the shed, and closing the door, they both ran for the shelter of the porch as a torrent of rain descended on them. Quickly retrieving his gun and gifts from the porch, Cory followed Annie into the unnaturally dark cabin. They were both laughing.

"Here!" she said, handing him a towel.

He stood by the door wiping the rain from his face while she scurried to get lights on and windows closed. At that moment, all of his senses were awakened by the intense smells of good food and the clean, cozy feel of home that emanated from her cabin. Even the fragrant and soft towel invited him to bury his face in it. He couldn't help smiling.

Annie teased him about the size of the carrots and thanked him for the fish, but it was clear that his gifts meant something special to her.

"I think this weather calls for a cup of hot chocolate with marshmallows," she suggested, grinning at him. "Please sit, Cory. We'll make a fire and pretend it's winter since my thermometer says the temperature has already dropped twenty-five degrees."

When Annie came into the living room with the steaming mugs and a plate of chewy caramel cookies, Cory had a small fire burning steadily. She slipped off her shoes and tucking her legs under her, she nestled into a large chair next to the fireplace. They sat in silence while the metal roof of the cabin reverberated with the ping of hail and the sky flashed with lightning and thunder. Soft instrumental music played from a radio on the table near Annie's chair and nothing more could make Cory feel so peaceful.

"You know I can't let you return to your cabin in this

weather, Cory," she stated simply, finally breaking their silence. "You'll have to stay, have supper with me, and remain here for the night. This is going to be a long and serious storm, if the weathermen are the least bit correct in their prediction."

"I can't stay, Annie," he said, sitting up from his relaxed position. "I came to get some information and then I need to head home."

She was already shaking her head before he finished speaking and he knew the argument was in her favor as he listened to the increasing wind and rain. How could he argue with her? Common sense told him that she was right and, at the moment, he did not want to give up the comfort he felt leaning against a mound of pillows on the floor in front of the fireplace with a mug of delicious cocoa and the dog by his side. As she took tiny sips of the steaming beverage, she studied him.

"Are you going to tell me about those bruises on your face?" she finally asked.

Cory looked up from the mesmerizing flames in the fireplace. "I had an opportunity to meet ALL of Jenny's brothers," he said with a grin. "Only Gobb and I had a difference of opinion. In fact, that's why I came to see you. He claims the trees they were cutting were on THEIR land, not my dad's. Since I was there also to cut trees, I need to know who was trespassing."

Without responding, Annie set her cocoa down and moved to the large bookcase on the opposite wall. After a few moments, she removed a spiral-bound book and came back to the chair, paging as she walked.

"Oh,...I need to know your father's first name. I'm assuming the last is the same as yours."

"Michael," he responded quickly, glancing up at her in time to see her shiver. "Annie, you're cold. Should I build up the fire?"

"No. No, I'm fine, Cory. It was just a little draft. Here, this is the information in the plat book about all our properties," she said as she snuggled back into her oversized chair.

Cory sat on the arm of the chair as they poured over the maps. Since he had constantly carried a compass and pedometer with him calculating the directions and distances every time he entered the woods, he could now determine over whose property they had fought. When he pointed to the spot where they had been cutting the trees yesterday, Cory felt disappointment. On the small map it appeared that they were on the very edge of both properties—the Redlam's and the Wharton's.

"I'm sorry, Cory," Annie said slowly, "but, it looks like you would need a surveyor to decide whose property that is." As she closed the book, she went on, "Although the Wharton boys have earned a reputation for being rather intimidating, I know from things Jenny tells me that they really aren't bad boys. Actually, several of them aren't really boys anymore; they're men."

Cory moved back to the floor and laughed. "And, what makes a boy into a man, Annie?" he asked.

Her quick response stunned him. "Well, it certainly isn't age, Cory. Some boys never become men." Annie shifted her gaze to the fire and a sadness came over her beautiful face. Speaking as though she was thinking out loud she continued. "I believe a boy becomes a man when he learns to forgive…to love…to be brave…to care about others…to persevere…and to be honest."

"Now, you're talking about my dad," he said proudly.

Annie was staring at him. He could feel her gaze and when he turned to look at her, the sadness in her eyes stirred his emotions. Suddenly he cared deeply that she would be happy.

"You love your dad very much, don't you," she stated

softly. "Please tell me about him."

For the next two hours, Cory spoke about his dad, their life together, his mother's death, what he could remember about her, his school, his friends, and even football. Annie seemed to devour every word, laughing with him about some of the stories and sympathizing with him on others. She was a good listener and it seemed so easy to tell her things that he would have told no other person. He was totally honest about his argument with his dad over football, but he could not bring himself to mention his love of classical guitar music. Cory could not bear the thought that she would disapprove or worse yet, that she might scoff at the silly idea of him playing classical music. Finally, aware of his monopoly of the conversation, he simply stopped talking and they continued to sit quietly watching the fire.

It was still raining very hard when Annie began heating a large pot of venison stew and more thunder and lightning came with the sweep of a second storm that hit them at supper time. But not much ever spoiled Cory's appetite and he ate Annie's stew, biscuits, fruit salad, and raspberry pie like this was his last meal.

The evening hours were gone before Cory realized it and although Annie offered him a bedroom, he chose to sleep right there in front of the fire with Brute, who was either an unusually friendly dog, or one who had taken a special liking to him. She tucked Cory in with extra blankets and retired to her room just as the storms seemed to lessen in intensity.

When it was time to go home the next morning, Cory was reluctant to leave Annie. During a hot breakfast of bacon and eggs, something he had not had for almost two months, he noticed a sadness in her and knew that something in her life had been seriously broken. Whatever it was, he wished with all his heart that he could fix it for her.

She stood on the steps, watching him as he left the clearing and stepped into the woods. He never looked back, but it hurt him to leave her. Cory saw her as a strong woman, capable of taking care of herself and others. He had learned that she successfully hunted deer and small game each fall, did many of her own simple repairs, planted a garden each year, and gathered enough wood to keep her cabin warm all winter. And yet, there were times when she seemed like an injured child. Then suddenly HE felt like the adult wanting to care for HER. With sudden awareness, he realized how much Annie meant to him.

It was late morning when he reached his cabin and, after checking the place for any storm damage, he immediately tackled the job of splitting his logs for his troughs. As the sky continued to clear, the temperature came back to the normal summer high, and the humidity rose with it. The work was slow and exhausting. Cory had promised himself that the project had to be done by the time his father arrived. However, the last time they spoke, circumstances had pushed that date back about two weeks. To Cory's surprise, he found that he was disappointed with the news. Now that his father knew where he was, the prospect of the two of them spending the last of the summer together had been very appealing. The new situation meant that it would be August before he arrived. However, that DID mean he had more time to get things ready.

With a huge sandwich and a warm but still refreshing can of soda from Annie, Cory abandoned his work and headed to the lake early that evening. Despite its spring-fed source of cold, fresh water, the sun was slowly taking over and the water was getting warmer every day. He swam across the lake and back before pulling himself onto the dock to eat.

The sun was already low in the sky when Cory saw movement across the lake. He watched as Jenny waded into the shallow edge and then dove into the dropoff. She was a good swimmer and he watched her graceful strokes as she headed his way. Apparently she was in the habit of swimming across the lake and back as he had and he guessed that she had not seen him lying on his stomach on the dock. To prevent frightening her, he waited until she was at least fifteen yards from him before he spoke.

"Come on up, Jenny. I might be a little demanding about my property, but I am willing to let others use it."

His words stopped her in mid stroke, but in a moment she recovered her surprise.

"Hi, Cory. Actually, I promised my dad that I'd be back before the sun set and I can see that it will be a race to beat it. Otherwise he'll just send out the 'platoon'," she joked, "and you know how they can be." She started to swim away and then called over her shoulder, "I'd like a rain check, if I can have one?"

"Sure, anytime," he shouted back.

As Cory stood up to leave he saw a fairly large animal moving into the brush on the opposite shore. Did Jenny have a dog? A big tan one?

"Jenny!" he hollered loudly. "Do you have a dog with you?"

She stopped swimming and swung around in the middle of the lake. "What?" she shouted as she treaded water.

"Do…you…have…a…large…tan…dog?"

"No," she shouted back. "Why?"

"Stay where you are," he commanded before diving into the lake. When he surfaced, he could see that she was continuing to swim toward the opposite shore. Burning as little energy as possible while thrusting his body forward with each stroke, he actually reached her a few yards from shore.

"Wait, Jenny! There was a large tan animal, not a deer, right here a few minutes ago. I saw too little of it to know just what it was, but I know that there have been wolves in the area lately."

"Look, I'm fine. I can take care of myself," Jenny said forcefully as she stepped out of the lake. "What you saw could easily be a deer and wolves are usually gray or black or even white."

He followed her onto the shore sweeping his gaze from side to side keeping his senses alert. "Let me walk you…"

"Absolutely not!" she stated emphatically, turning on him as she toweled herself. "I am quite capable of taking myself home and besides, I have enough trouble with those brothers of mine. Nobody in my family is a wimp!"

Cory was stunned. He had no intention of insulting her or making her angry, but what he had seen worried him. He knew deer and was familiar enough with their movements to know that this had not been one. Still confused and concerned, Cory watched as Jenny strode purposely down the trail, into the woods, and out of sight. In the dim light of late evening, Cory checked the ground where he had seen the animal and his worry increased when he discovered paw prints larger than his closed fists. These were not the prints of a bear, nor the dog-like prints of a wolf or coyote. These were cat paws and NO domestic cat would ever be this large.

That week Cory returned to the lake each afternoon when he needed a break from the construction of his water system. He was constantly alert to the presence of animal tracks around his own creek and he checked both sides of the lake each time he went. Although he found no new cat prints among the many deer, raccoon, and even bear prints, the image of the tan animal moving into the brush on Jenny's side of the lake worried him. After a great deal of thought and research through the animal books in the cabin, Cory could come to only one conclusion. This was a cougar/puma/mountain lion. Of course, he knew they were not common to this area, and, of course, he knew it sounded impossible. But then wolves had not been seen in this part of the country for decades either—until now. The more he reviewed the sighting in his mind, the more he was convinced of what he saw.

He was frightened for Jenny. She obviously spent a great deal of time alone in the woods, walking to the lake, picking berries, and hiking. Hadn't she come all the way to his place alone?

On Thursday, Cory stepped back from his water project and decided that one more pine tree would finish the job. Gathering his gear and grabbing one of the guns, he set off for the "woods of undetermined ownership."

Crossing the creek, Cory began to laugh out loud at the irony that hit him. After his attempts to avoid them, he was suddenly hoping to run into Jenny's brothers so he could warn them about the tracks he had found, the sighting, and his conclusion. Despite the difficult time they gave her, they certainly would want to protect her against a serious threat like this. Wouldn't they?

The perfectly straight, exact-sized pine that Cory cut, came down easily and it was trimmed and harnessed in record time. Slipping the leather strap over his body in order to pull the log with his waist, he picked up the gun, slung the bag of tools over his shoulder, and set out for the cabin, when a voice stopped him.

"I thought my brother told you to get off our property."

Cory released the harness and turned around to see Jenny's brother, Pooter, carrying a chainsaw and pulling a small sled with thick wooden runners. Apparently they were still gathering and splitting wood.

"Look," Cory said wearily, "I'm not looking for trouble. The fact is, this land is on the border of our properties and it will take a surveyor to determine where the boundaries are. Until then, we're obviously both taking the trees," he stated honestly. "Actually, I was hoping to run into one of you," he continued. "I have seen a large tan animal with huge cat prints in the same area of the lake where Jenny swims. It has to be a mountain lion and I thought someone in your family should know about the danger."

Before Cory had finished, he saw the grin of disbelief on Pooter's face and he waited for the laughter which followed quickly.

"Gosh, would you like me to carry your big gun for you and protect you on the way home?" Pooter asked sarcastically as he started to walk toward Cory.

It was clear that Cory was wasting his breath, so he pulled up the harness and began pulling the log toward home. Pooter followed with a constant stream of teasing.

"You know? I could watch your back as you walk so that the great big kitty can't get you. Or maybe we should call the sheriff's department and get help? I can see your knees shaking. Don't worry! I'll protect you."

Were Jenny's brothers all morons like this one? What must it be like in their household? Since he was an only child, Cory had no idea what it was like to be teased all the time, except for what he gathered from his friends' families, but this was eroding his patience rapidly.

As distracted as he was by all of Pooter's rambling, Cory lost track of the path around the swampy area and discovered it too late. Stepping too close to the bog, he suddenly was pitched to the side as he slid from a stable footing to the muck of the swamp. In an attempt to save the shotgun, he dropped the bag of tools and broke his fall with the right side of his body. Muck splashed all over him while his left arm held the gun in the air.

Pooter's immediate and raucous laughter was sucking out the very last of Cory's patience. Salvaging the tools and gun, he placed them a few yards away on high ground and returned to pull out his log, brushing the excess mud from his face and body. As he bent to pull the harness out of the muck, he noticed how solid and round the pieces of the bog were—like small basketballs and scooping one up he threw it with every bit of force he could muster directly at Pooter about ten yards away.

It caught him high on his chest, spattering mud all over his face. Before he knew what had hit him, Cory whipped a second ball of mud, and then a third. Running from the onslaught, Pooter staggered from four more direct hits to his back. Cory was relentless and without a single miss, he continued to fire them until Pooter was well out of range.

So much for trying to protect Jenny, Cory thought as he sat and plucked his guitar that evening. He smiled as he thought of the sight he must have been after falling into the bog. Good thing she had not been there to see it.

Because circumstances demanded it, he had heated water for a real bath to remove the smell of the swamp and now after a full and satisfying meal, he felt the peace of his cabin. He really loved it here. Would his father love it too? Or would he insist that they leave? Cory hoped not. He wanted Annie to get to meet his dad. After all, they were the two most important people in his life at the moment.

Chapter 6

Cory's water project was successfully completed to the extent that water was available at his doorstep whenever he wanted it. Along with the troughs and the water wheel, he had fashioned an outdoor shower from an old sprinkling can. The sun warmed the two-gallon can of water on a platform suspended above his head. When a person wanted to get wet, you merely pulled a rope attached to the spout which swung the can into a pouring position. A quick soaping and a refreshing rinse completed the process of showering. The whole platform was enclosed with the extra bed sheets that had covered the ruined and discarded mattresses. It was a great shower. However, as the summer moved into the third week of July, Cory fell into a regular pattern of bathing in the lake at the end of each day.

After a particularly busy day of picking black berries, cutting the lawn, and cleaning the cabin, Cory walked to the lake earlier than usual. A long easy swim completely around the lake revealed a consistent dropoff along the perimeter, and he realized that there were only two places that a dock could possibly be constructed—Jenny's side of the lake and his. It made him smile each time he thought of "her side of the lake," as though he had given her a piece of his property.

Pulling himself onto his dock, Cory remembered the cat tracks and wondered if Pooter had even mentioned it to her. Maybe it was better if he didn't, since neither of them believed him anyway. They would just laugh and joke about how stupid he was. As he lay in the sun half asleep, Cory was suddenly aware of how much it would hurt to hear Jenny laughing at him.

For almost two months, Cory had kept the secret of his love for music. Each time he played the guitar, he made sure that he was alone and had stopped playing at the lake after learning that Jenny frequently swam there. With a family of big, tough brothers, she would certainly make fun of his "whimpy" guitar.

Now, a jerk of the dock brought Cory out of his thoughts in time to see Jenny pulling herself up the ladder.

"You said I could have a rain-check," she stated firmly as she stepped onto the dock.

He smiled. "Of course, welcome to the Redlam Estates!"

She took the half of his beach towel that he offered and spread it out to lie down.

"The lake is really warm today," she said in her most casual tone.

He could tell something was on her mind so he remained silent. For a long time, the silence hung in the air. Then, raising herself to lean on her arms, she looked at him and said, "I'm sorry I was mad the other evening when you offered to walk me home. I know that you were only worried about my safety and I should have been grateful. I'm sorry!"

Cory stared at her, trying to read the sincerity in her eyes and finally he nodded without speaking. They lapsed into silence. Cory felt relaxed and comfortable just soaking up the sun after his refreshing swim.

Jenny finally swung her legs around and sat up. "Cory, do you play football at your high school?" she asked innocently.

Here we go, he thought, already feeling the anger rise. Good thing she doesn't know about my music or we'd all have a good laugh, he thought sarcastically. Attempting to hold his temper, Cory swung around to a sitting position, hugging his knees to his chest as he stared toward the lake.

"No!" he responded rudely without looking at her or explaining.

"Look!" She spoke with anger surfacing in her own voice. "I didn't mean to ask you such a touchy question. It was only because Pooter has been raving about your ability to throw that I thought to ask. That's called conversation!" She spit the words out angrily as she stood up.

Rising to face her, Cory spoke accusingly. "I'll bet you're one of those girls that only dates the captain of the football team."

Anger flared in her eyes. "Hardly!" she shouted. "That would be Pooter!"

In one swift and graceful movement, Jenny turned and dove into the water. Cory could see that she was swimming under water as far as possible from the dock before surfacing. She never looked back and he knew she would not respond if he shouted that he was sorry he had angered her. And he was!

Why couldn't they get along? Why was there always some misunderstanding between them? Why did he take offense at everything she said? The subject of football had become such an argument with everyone—his dad, the coaches at school, his friends, and now Jenny. He hadn't meant that to happen.

As Jenny entered the path on the other side of the lake, he picked up his towel and headed to the cabin. So Pooter was captain of the football team. That figures, Cory thought. Then he wondered if each of the older brothers had taken their turns as captain. The possibility was highly likely. As Cory walked along, he was forced to smile when he thought of Pooter actually bragging about him. But the smile was quickly erased when he remembered Jenny's anger.

As weather patterns coursed through the summer months in the northwoods, they invariably alternated from hot, humid days to cold, wet periods. It was time for the cold and wet—four days of it! This was not a storm, only a low pressure system that had stalled in its movement, bringing a gloomy, overcast sky and lots of steady rain. Even the cabin voiced its disapproval with darkened walls and damp air bringing a sense of loneliness and sadness to Cory.

Remembering the time he had spent at Annie's when he had felt such peace and contentment during the storm, made him realize how much he wished she was with him now. He was eager to have his dad meet her. Although his father had never expressed an interest in remarrying, Cory would not have objected. And, although she was much too old for him, Cory would have welcomed a mother like Annie.

As Cory spent the rainy days inside the cabin getting it ready for the arrival of his father, he found himself frequently lost in deep thought. It shocked him to realize that he knew so little about his dad. Most teenagers were not very aware of their parents on a personal basis but he had always assumed that being an only child and having a single parent would cause both of them to be more attentive to each other. But Cory was overwhelmed by the fact that he had no idea what foods his dad liked best, what books he read, what relaxed him, or what he disliked. The only sure thing was his father's love of sports.

Cory tried to picture his dad and as the vague image took shape, it frightened him. What kind of son was he that he knew so little about his dad? Tall, muscular yet thin, blond hair like Cory's and that was the extent of the picture he could compose of his father. Were there no scars, no distinctive features that Cory had paid attention to? If Cory knew so little about his father, why should his father know anything about him or understand his love of music and his desire to play the guitar?

With a sense of excitement, Cory realized suddenly that they had a chance to start over. His dad would be here in less than a week and they could spend the rest of the summer getting to know each other. He was eager to show his dad the innovations he had made and the skills he had learned. And Annie! He wanted his dad to meet Annie.

Rigorously Cory returned to the job of readying the cabin. He had been collecting pine cones for the past month which he now stuffed into a large burlap sack. Two of the sacks placed end to end on a bed spring would become a mattress. Covering the sacks with blankets made a sturdy, yet not totally uncomfortable bed. His father could sleep on the only good mattress. With renewed energy Cory spent the dreary days preparing for his father's arrival. Because he was not fully ready for a big debate about his music, he hung the guitar on the wall of the summer kitchen out of plain sight.

Since the weather had prevented Cory from seeing Jenny, the unspoken apology that he carried, grew heavier with each passing day. He had been unfair and rude to her at the lake and she deserved an apology.

In the evening of the fourth day of rain, the sky promised a change with a startling sunset that peaked between the purple and pink layers of clouds. The rain had finally ended and the smells of the wet fields and trees were intense. Cory strolled to the creek, inspecting his water system as he slowly walked along. As was expected, the creek was swollen and the ground saturated. What wasn't expected were the large paw prints of a cat that Cory found at the edge of the stream. So the puma ranges this far from the lake, he thought. Quickly he returned to the cabin to get his small pocket camera. Grabbing a tape measure, he hurried back to the creek, placed the measure over the width of the track and snapped a digital picture. This time he would have proof of the cat to show Jenny.

Annie had said that the Wharton home was about six miles south of Cory's place. With compass and pedometer, camera and hunting knife, Cory left the cabin right after breakfast, intending to check the lake shore for more cat prints on his way. Certainly Jenny's parents would consider the danger to be serious now, even if the brothers made fun of him. However, when more prints were found at the lake, Cory took several extra pictures to strengthen his proof.

Once he was past the lake, the unfamiliar terrain posed a problem for him. It took concentration and numerous glances to the pedometer and compass to step around fallen trees and circle the swamps and still remain on a straight course, until he found the path that Jenny must be using to get to the lake. Crossing the east fork of the logging road, Cory resumed his pace on the path which extended through another pine plantation and an hour later, he left the woods to see a two-story farmhouse, a large red barn, and a metal-roofed machine shed.

Chickens scattered in front of him as he passed the barn to get to the house. A woman sitting on the porch had not yet seen him. Just beyond the door of the barn, Cory came to a halt as a familiar voice taunted him.

"Well! Look who's here! Weren't you afraid to come all this way with the big kitty out there somewhere?"

The voice could not be ignored. Slowly Cory turned to find Gobb leaning lazily against the door frame. There was nothing to say so they stood there glaring at one another until Coonsey and Truck came out of the barn to join their brother.

"Hey! The trespasser!" one of them said. "See any

more kitties? Wow! Get a look at that butcher knife he carries. Bet every wild creature in the woods is scared of him."

All three of them were bent in laughter when a woman's voice gave an order.

"Okay, boys. That's enough!"

Cory turned to see the petite woman from the porch wiping her hands on an apron that covered her jeans and T-shirt. She extended a hand and said, "Welcome to the Wharton home. I'm Doris."

"Cory Redlam, ma'am," he explained as he shook her hand. "I'd like to speak to Jenny."

Whistles, jeers, and catcalls echoed behind him. "Little Jenny has a boyfriend and he's here to protect her from that ferooooooooocious kitty."

Mrs. Wharton stepped around Cory with anger flashing in her eyes and hands on her hips. Apparently the message was received. All three sons became silent instantly and turned to go back to their work, but not until Cory heard one of them say, "Whimp!"

"I must apologize, Cory, for the behavior of my ADOLESCENT sons," Mrs. Wharton explained as she grabbed him by the arm and propelled him toward the porch. "They are so used to teasing each other that they forget to control themselves with other people."

As they ascended the steps, Cory repeated his request to speak with Jenny. Mrs. Wharton motioned for him to sit and she resumed the snipping of beans into a huge wooden bowl. "I'm sorry," she said, "but Jenny went off with some of her friends this afternoon. They're shopping for school clothes already." She laughed. "I'll have to drag the boys at gun point to get some new clothes, but girls are so easy. Can I give her a message?"

"No. I…guess my apology will have to wait."

Mrs. Wharton looked up from her work and raised

an eyebrow questioningly. Cory did not respond to her inquiry and simply changed the subject.

"Mrs. Wharton, I have been finding large cat prints all around the lake where Jenny swims, and I believe it is a cougar or mountain lion." He waited for the ridicule. Nothing came. A frown appeared instead. "I have a picture of the prints," he stated as he pulled his digital camera from his pocket and showed her the pictures. Her frown deepened as she studied them.

"I'd like my husband to see these, but he's not home now. He teaches at the local high school and had meetings today."

"Keep the camera for a few days," Cory said generously. "I seem to be running into some member of your family from time to time anyway. Someone will return it to me."

She accepted the camera that he held out to her and thanked him, promising that it would get back to him by the end of the week. Before she finished speaking, Pooter appeared at the door.

"Hey! You're just the guy I want to see," he exclaimed, stepping onto the porch.

Cory stiffened, expecting a fight. After all, the last time he saw Pooter was when he pelted him with mud.

Sensing a problem, Mrs. Wharton stepped between them. "Alex, this is Cory," she stated, calmly. "Cory, this is my youngest son, and the brightest, and the most pleasant of the boys," she said pointedly.

Pooter smiled. "There's no problem, Ma. I get the message. I just want to talk to the guy." With that, he slipped his arm over Cory's shoulder and walked him buddy-like down the steps and out onto the lawn. Cory was still waiting for this new-found camaraderie to disintegrate when the sales pitch started.

"Every August a bunch of guys get together in our

alfalfa field and play a rousing game of football," Pooter began. "My dad and the football coach from school, in a friendly game of rivalry, pit one team against the other. They each have to pull their own team together from wherever they can," he explained enthusiastically. "But here comes the best part," he said as he swung around to face Cory. "The winning team spends a whole day at a fancy resort about thirty miles from here where you can water ski, swim, run jet skis, ride horses, shoot skeet, and eat anything you want—all free!" Almost out of breath, Pooter added, "We could use a guy with your throwing arm. How about it?" When only silence answered his question, Pooter shrugged his shoulders and attempted to dismiss their prior disagreement.

Cory sighed and stared at Pooter's expectant face. Finally he shook his head and said, "I don't play football."

It wasn't the look that crossed Pooter's face or the expression in his eyes that bothered Cory. It was the multitude of labels like coward, whimp, softy, nerd, and weakling that he knew were going through Pooter's thoughts that really tore him apart. He hated the labeling.

"What? Anyone who throws like you do can be on a team. Are you afraid?" Pooter was getting angry and Cory knew the futility of this argument. Therefore he simply turned and walked away.

"Wait a minute!" Pooter shouted. "What's the matter with you? Are you just another whimp?"

That did it! By now Cory was seething inside. What right does anyone have to label people weaklings just because they don't want to conform. How much easier life would be, he thought, if he simply played their stupid game. That thought and his anger, conspired to push the words from his mouth before he realized he had said them. "All right!" he shouted back angrily, "I'll play your stupid game!"

As he entered the woods he heard Pooter yell, "We practice here on Thursday!"

Cory never looked back. His frustration fueled his stride and he crossed the logging road in record time trying to outrun his jumbled thoughts. Why not play football? Maybe his dad was right. What's the big deal? So what if it's simply not his choice? Who cares? Play the stupid game his senior year and get everybody off his back. Why not?

The questions fell over each other in his mind. But that was the problem. They were questions, not answers. Cory was so very tired of fighting everybody, and now it was the Wharton brothers. Did he really have to prove his bravery to others before he was accepted as himself?

That evening Cory attempted to regain the peace and contentment that the cabin and its surroundings so frequently brought him. For three hours he sat on the porch picking the strings of his guitar, practicing scales and ending with the Latin rhythms that he loved so well. The setting sun, as if in sympathy with his mood, rewarded him with one of the most beautiful displays of gold, orange, yellow, and tinges of pink scattered through a band of clouds resting just above the horizon.

Thursday was a beautiful, dry day when Cory left for the Wharton property. While he trekked through the woods, he continued the mental debate about football and before his choice was even formed into words, he was aware that he would be playing football this coming school year. He had come to the cabin to spend a summer without arguing the subject and found only MORE people to fight on the issue. In one month he would be returning home and to school. That month he hoped to spend peacefully with his dad and that meant that his choice between music and football had to be settled now. He WOULD play! The choice would be football!

By the time Cory reached the Wharton home, he felt lighter and more free than he had in months. How could his decision have weighed so heavily on him? Was he just being so incredibly stubborn? No! Music really was his first choice. But this would not be a big thing unless he made it so. After all, he played football often in his physical education classes and it was not a problem then. He would simply think of it as something he was instructed to do.

When Cory approached, Mrs. Wharton was standing in the yard scattering feed for the chickens while they fought over each piece of grain. The boys were already gathering in the field when Mr. Wharton came down the steps from the house to be introduced. Unlike his sons, he was a thin man, although tall.

"Well," he said, motioning Cory to follow him, "Alex tells us you have a great arm for football so let's see what you can do."

With a total of just eleven players, Mr. Wharton took his team through the rigors of a strenuous practice following the introductions. Consistent with his prior efforts at football, Cory played exceptionally well, receiving praise even from Gobb, although he was sure the hits from some of the brothers were cemented with a little extra zeal—payback for their dislike of him. Since the day of the mud fight, Pooter, however, had displayed a small amount of respect toward Cory despite their disagreements.

Flipping towels from one to the other to wipe the sweat from their faces, and guzzling water, they sprawled on the lawn waiting for the decisions of their coach. The practice had been spirited and as Mr. Wharton read their names and assigned their positions, enthusiasm flowed among them. Cory sat on the ground opposite Pooter and when Cory was selected for the position of quarterback, he looked at Pooter in surprise.

While the rest of the team moved to the porch for the lemonade, grilled hamburgers, and salad, Cory tried to read the expression on Pooter's face. "Look…" he started to say when Pooter interrupted him.

"The best man for the job, gets it," he stated simply. "My dad is a good coach and we have a good team. You'll make a good quarterback and I'll be a GREAT receiver!" He grinned and Cory shook the hand that he extended to him.

Dressed in red shorts and a white tank top with her silky brunette hair swinging loosely around her face, Jenny joined them on the porch for the picnic. It was obvious that she was well-liked by the others. Hoping to speak to her later in order to unload the apology that he had been carrying around with him since their mutual anger at the lake, Cory mentally rehearsed what he wanted to say. However, as the meal progressed, he read the flashes of anger in her eyes and wondered about the intense looks she gave him.

Following him off the porch, and before he had a moment to apologize, Jenny launched into her complaint.

"Thank you so much, Mr. Redlam," she fumed sarcastically, "for trying to protect me from that ferocious beast in the woods." She had moved one hand dramatically to her forehead as the damsels in distress often did in the old silent movies and then she continued with hands on her hips and a defiant stare at Cory. "Thanks to you, I am no longer allowed to even enter the woods, let alone swim at the lake." She spun around and started for the house, flinging the last words over her shoulder. "Try to remember something. We Whartons can take care of ourselves!"

Cory stood there in silent amazement. If it was

possible, he would have enjoyed pulling the apology from his head, tearing it to shreds and scattering it all over the lawn. In confusion and frustration he left the Wharton property with his camera that Jenny thrust angrily into his hand before striding away.

He needed a vacation from the Whartons. Maybe tomorrow he would spend the entire day picking blackberries with the bears. Getting along with them would be so much easier.

Chapter 7

Several times during the night, Cory woke to the howling of wolves or coyotes. He had never seen either one except for their tracks and he knew that both would not roam the same territory, but since the prints he found appeared so large, he assumed they were wolves rather than coyotes. Sleep had come with difficulty after his unhappy encounter with Jenny and the thought of his father arriving tomorrow kept him awake now.

Would his father actually be willing to live here for the month of August when he was used to fine dining and fancy hotels? As proud as Cory was of his water system and shower, the real question was whether his dad would think it was silly. Cory was worried. He couldn't bear the thought of having to give up this last month and go home. For him, THIS was home. He loved it here and if it was his choice, he would stay for the winter.

For a long time, Cory lay on his stomach looking out the two windows of the loft. He could smell the cool breeze of the night air through the open windows and he thought about his life here in the north woods. Then, sometime around three o'clock he fell soundly asleep only to be rudely awakened at five by the riveting sounds of a woodpecker on the metal flashing of the roof.

By eight, Cory had checked the water supply three times; caught four fish from the stream; picked a small pail of blackberries; gathered carrots and beans from the garden; and squeezed the juice from a small sack of chokecherries, which when mixed with water and Annie's gift of sugar, made a tolerably refreshing drink.

When Cory had spoken to his dad last evening, his father reported that he would rent a Jeep and fill a cooler with milk, eggs, meat, and other items of perishable food to supplement Cory's meager rations. Because he did not expect his father before noon and waiting patiently was impossible, Cory hiked to the lake. He was relieved to find no new cougar tracks and yet the lack of them caused him to question his belief that a dangerous cat existed in the area. Maybe Jenny's anger was justified. Did he really spoil her summer as she implied?

With the eager anticipation of a little kid, Cory sat in the rocker on the porch at eleven o'clock watching the old car tracks that had led him to the cabin two months ago and now were only visible where he had cut the grass up to the woods. From there the path of the tracks could be detected only where Cory had traveled it back to the gate, hacking at the saplings and brush to clear it. Now he stared at the farthest spot where he knew the first sign of the Jeep would appear.

Exactly at noon, an open, military Jeep bounced through the brush into the clearing, although Cory had been listening to the groan of its engine long before he saw it. Getting to his feet, he stood and watched its movement over the rough terrain. Not wanting to seem foolishly eager, he waited until his dad had turned the key and stepped from the vehicle before he came down the steps.

Cory smiled as he noted the tall, athletic, but older duplicate of himself. From the hiking boots to the cargo shorts and polo, it looked as though his dad was prepared to stay at least the month. He grinned as he stepped toward his dad and their eyes locked.

Suddenly, the grin dissolved. Cory found himself looking into the SECOND pair of the most intensely blue eyes he had ever seen. Stunned and confused, he stood immobile while the strong arms that wrapped around him, as they had always done since he was little, nearly sucked the breath out of him.

"You're looking good and healthy," his father said as he released him.

"Thanks... you too," Cory managed to mumble, while the name "Annie" tore through his brain in a frenzy of jumbled thoughts.

Cory stumbled through the motions of helping his dad carry in all his gear and supplies, while his mind raced. Was this all a joke? Why hadn't he noticed his dad's incredible blue eyes before? Could two people with the same amazing eyes be total strangers? Was it possible that they were related? No! That couldn't be possible! She said her family was dead. Her son was dead! She said so! With great difficulty Cory tried to close his mind to the disturbing questions.

Setting the last bag of groceries on the table, his dad turned and gently placed a hand on Cory's shoulder, looking at him questioningly. "Is something the matter, Cory?" his father asked. "You look upset."

Forcing a grin and giving a poor imitation of a laugh, Cory pushed aside the mental chaos that threatened to engulf him, knowing that something was very wrong but wanting to speak as calmly as possible. "I'm fine, dad. I've...just been looking forward to your coming and it seems so great that you're finally here."

His father smiled and nodded. "This will be fun, Cory. We'll have a good time and, now that my business problem is settled, I'll be able to spend a whole month with you. I regret that my work has kept me away so much. But we'll make the best of the time we have."

While Cory showed him where things were and they packed the supplies away, he noted the sadness in his dad's eyes as he looked over the cabin. "You must have worked pretty hard to get the place cleaned up after all these years. What did it look like when you got here?" he asked.

Describing his arrival in June and showing his father all the things he had accomplished, including the water system and the building of his docks, took most of the afternoon and diverted Cory's thoughts from Annie to the immediate moment. She had become more important than he realized and it would hurt to learn that she might have kept secrets from him that he had a right to know.

Michael Redlam was astounded at his son's ingenuity in fashioning the shower and constructing the docks at both the creek and the lake and he grinned in amazement when Cory started his water wheel. Then, he watched in fascination as Cory caught a fish in less than a few minutes with his "strainer technique." Because of the steady flow of the water, any fish traveling upstream was momentarily suspended in an unmoving position right at the end of the small dock. If the kitchen strainer was placed in the stream with its open end facing downstream, fish invariably arrived in that perfect spot long enough to be scooped from the water.

As they hiked to the lake that evening for a refreshing swim, Cory told his dad about the neighbors to the south and the disagreement about the dock. After explaining the nicknames of the Wharton brothers and describing them, he told each of the stories of his encounters with them including the paw prints that he believed to be from a cougar. To his surprise and satisfaction, his dad did not find the theory of the cougar to be funny or worthy of dismissal and he promised to question the Forestry Department about possible sightings when he checked on the boundaries of his property in a day or so.

Deliberately, Cory avoided the subjects of music and football. Although he had decided days ago to play football his senior year, he wasn't ready yet to tell his dad.

Like two young kids they raced each other across the lake and back, then lay exhausted on the dock, watching families of geese and the almost grown goslings paddle in and out of the reeds to feed. So many questions burned on Cory's tongue and with difficulty he kept most of them to himself. Rolling over on his back and staring at the clouds he finally trusted himself to ask, "Dad. In your opinion, what makes a boy into a man?"

At first Cory thought there wasn't going to be an answer, but eventually his father rolled over too and slowly responded. "Well, it isn't age." He paused and seemed to be reciting from memory. "I think a boy becomes a man when he learns to care about others, to be brave, to love, to be honest, to work hard, and to forgive." He smiled and laughed as though the words had flung him back into another time and place, where memories were filled with happiness. "My mother taught me that," he said with pride.

THOSE WERE ANNIE'S WORDS!

Cory's mouth felt dry and stiff as he tried to form the sentence for his request. "Tell me about your mother," he said with feeling.

There was only silence for what seemed like a very long time.

"I'm sorry, Cory. She's dead. And it's really too painful to talk about her," his dad explained, getting up from the dock. "Maybe we should be heading back to the cabin."

Neither of them spoke as they walked single file through the woods on the path that had been worn down by Cory's frequent trips to the lake. He was feeling hurt and somewhat angry that his father refused to talk about his own mother. After all, he had a right to know something about HIS grandmother, whether she was dead, or not! And, now that he thought about it, his father never spoke of Cory's mother either. It wasn't fair. He was seventeen and not a baby. He had a right to learn about them and then decide for himself whether he would choose to remember them or not. No wonder he could recall so few things about his mother. They never spoke of her.

With the arrival of August, each night the sky darkened earlier than the night before and already the sound of the leaves rustling in the wind carried a note of fall. Tonight was one of those evenings that held the warnings of the first freeze and the temperature was dropping rapidly from the heat of the day as they wound their way from the lake.

Cory had no intention of mentioning Annie and, because she had become so important to him, he struggled to prevent himself from accidentally speaking of her. He needed to talk to her, alone and soon! He feared that she had not been truthful with him. No two people could have such similar eyes and mannerisms. Each time his father moved or spoke, Cory was reminded of Annie.

For the next two days, father and son hiked the property, swam at the lake, rode the logging trails with the Jeep, and played sports with makeshift equipment. A broken tree branch made a good bat, rocks and pinecones served as balls, and a smooth, round rock from the creek wedged into the split end of a piece of branch and tied with leather shoelaces made a great golf club. Even though the gear resulted in exceptionally challenging games, the competition and laughter made their efforts worthwhile and, in the long run, it seemed to be more fun.

Michael Redlam's persuasive arguments against surviving on food from nature while he was there, convinced Cory that he needed meat and milk products along with his wilderness diet of fish, fruit, and natural greens. Therefore, his father suggested a trip into the town of Woodville, which was also the county seat, to get groceries and check on their property borders, but Cory declined the invitation to go along, pointing out the neglected lawn and his need to cut it. The greater need, however, was to speak to Annie.

When the jeep disappeared into the natural camouflage of the woods on his dad's way to the logging road on Friday, Cory was already stepping off the porch in his hurry to get to Annie's. Today he hoped to untangle the mess of questions and bits of facts that had tormented him since his father's arrival. At almost a jogging pace the trip there and back would still take just under four hours and he must be back before his dad returned.

For the first time since Cory met Annie, the trip to her house was not enjoyable. A mixture of anger and sadness swept over him every time he came to the conclusion that she had lied to him. Then caution and a desire to be fair swayed him to other possibilities. It was the vicious circle of accusations and denials that twisted his thoughts and, in his haste, caused him to lose his way and forced him to backtrack twice. Of course, the growth of bushes, vines, and trees had steadily increased over the summer but they, too, seemed to conspire against him.

When finally he reached the lawn surrounding Annie's cabin, she was just closing and latching the door of her shed. He stopped and watched her lithe movements. When she turned and saw him, it was clear that her perceptive mind knew immediately that Cory had not come for a simple visit. He carried nothing in his hands as a small gift to her and his motionless stare revealed his unease.

"What's wrong, Cory?" she asked.

"We need to talk, Annie." The words came out hoarsely. Beautiful blue eyes stared at him.

"Come," she replied quietly, motioning toward the cabin.

He followed her, watching the swing of her thick, white braid as she mounted the stairs and held the door for him to enter.

"Would you like something to drink?" she asked hesitantly.

"No!" he replied bluntly. "And, I don't care to sit," he added, meaningfully.

"You're angry!" Annie said with a mixture of surprise and confusion in her voice. "Why?"

Suddenly realizing how unfair he was being, Cory shook his head and led her to a chair. She waited silently and expectantly for him to sit and explain.

"Annie," he began carefully. "I need to ask you some questions."

She nodded with a puzzled frown.

"About your family!" he added. "You said they were all dead. I need to know when and how they died." She looked away, but not before he saw the misery and despair in her eyes. He leaned forward and took one of her hand in a pleading gesture. "Are we…related?"

As she looked up, the pooled tears in her eyes slipped down her cheeks. Struggling with the smile that refused to fully form, she reached out and brushed his face with her fingers. "I hope so," she whispered. Pulling herself back into the corner of the chair, she slipped her feet under her legs and hugged herself as if she was cold.

Cory relaxed and waited patiently for Annie to explain. When she began, it came in a soft, halting voice that quivered with emotion.

"Twenty-four years ago,…on a Wednesday…in Spring,…my husband and I were on our way to Oregon…with our two beautiful children…when the car went off the road…and down an embankment." She paused to gain control, then slowly began again. "My husband, Steve, and my daughter, Amanda,…were killed upon impact at the bottom of the ravine." Fresh tears flowed down her face. She wiped them away with the back of her hand. "I was driving!" she moaned. " My son and I were both injured, but not critically." Misery clouded her eyes and the tormented memories filled her voice with anguish, pleading with him to let her stop.

Cory had never been intentionally cruel in his life, but he couldn't let her stop. He still didn't know the truth. Now, he sat silently, waiting for her to continue.

Grasping the control of her emotions, she went on. "I know that something went wrong with the car that day, but when I tried to explain that the brakes had not worked properly, the tests they ran seemed to prove otherwise." She frowned and confusion registered on her face. "Although I was never legally punished for the accident, it went into the record as 'inattentive driving'." She winced as she said it.

"I don't blame my son for hating me. I hated myself. He attended the funeral, packed his things and, at seventeen years of age, left home never to be seen or heard from again. I couldn't handle the losses—my wonderful husband, beautiful twelve-year-old daughter, and now my son. The looks of pity and blame that came from former friends and neighbors, and my own hatred of myself drove me to sell my house, buy this property, and build this cabin. Then, three years after the accident, I received a recall notice from the car manufacturer telling me to have the car serviced to correct a rare but proven malfunction of the brakes. By then, it was too late to redeem myself."

Annie sighed and shook her head slowly. "I may not have been legally punished," she said sadly, "but I have been punished in a thousand other ways. Isn't it punishment enough to have lost my soul mate, the only man I ever loved and my beautiful daughter? Isn't it enough that my seventeen-year-old son hated me for killing the father he loved above everything else in life? Isn't it enough that friends and neighbors viewed me as a careless woman who thoughtlessly killed half her family and endangered her son? Isn't it enough that my son refused to speak to me and left home as soon as he recovered from the accident, never to see me again." New tears engulfed her in misery as she buried her face in her hands and wept.

Cory knelt beside her chair and wrapped his arms around her. "Annie," he said, "your son's name."

Looking sadly into his eyes, she whispered, "Michael!"

A warmth spread over Cory. Annie was not just someone he admired and loved for the beautiful person she was. Annie was his Grandmother! He continued to sit with her until she calmed herself and could finally smile at him. He felt guilty for having tortured her by resurrecting the memories she had tried to bury. Finally, he took both her hands in his and looked into her eyes. "You know the truth, don't you," he stated. She smiled.

"You're my grandson, aren't you?"

He nodded. "I think so, but there are still a lot of questions that haven't been answered yet. Your last name is Winters and ours is Redlam. How is that explained?"

"Oh, Cory," Annie exclaimed as she stood up. "You don't understand how much Michael hated me for what happened. My guess is that he couldn't even tolerate the same name as mine and he changed it."

"But why wouldn't he have understood when the car company admitted their fault in the matter, since that cleared you of any responsibility for the accident?"

"By then, I no longer knew where he was. He didn't want any contact with me and it would have been very easy for him to disappear, so…he was never told! He doesn't know!" She frowned, then smiled and sighed. "How does he look, Cory? Is he well? Happy?"

"Yes, he's well and happy. At least, I think he's happy. He needs to know the truth about you."

"NO!" she pleaded. "Please don't tell him anything about me, Cory. I can't take any more hatred or anger. I have YOU now and he would take that from me too. Please keep this a secret from him. You don't understand how much he hates me. Promise me?"

He nodded and looked at his watch, stunned to see how late it was. He didn't want to leave Annie, but he needed to get back to the cabin before his father. As they walked across the lawn to the edge of the clearing, he reassured her several times that he would say nothing to his dad about her.

With that promise in his head, he hurried through the woods, running wherever he could to make it back to the cabin in time to cut the lawn. Luck was with him. It had taken much longer for his father to gather the property information that he needed and the jeep did not appear until well after four in the afternoon. By that time, Cory's flimsy excuse for not going with his dad was completed. The lawn was cut, and Cory had started cooking a large pot of soup with the vegetables from his garden.

Fresh meat and a small grill seemed to be the two most important items purchased by his father in town with a gallon of milk, chocolate chip cookies, and fresh fruit rating second. Not to be dismissed, however, were the chips, cheese, and soda, which were items that Cory had truly missed this summer. Maybe his father was right about living off the land. After all, isn't proving that you can do it, the most important point? And, reminding himself of the turkey eggs, fish, and water cress, he had certainly done that!

While Cory watched his dad expertly cooking the steaks on the grill, he considered bringing out his guitar and playing for him, but the last conversation that they had two months ago about his love of music had not gone well, and if he remembered correctly, it had ended in an angry exchange. Would it be worth the risk? The answer was no. So far the experience with his dad at the cabin had been nothing but pleasant. Why ruin that now.

Amazed at his father's restraint in avoiding the subject of football since he arrived, Cory wondered at the cause of it. Although Cory had decided two weeks ago that he WOULD be playing football his senior year, something held him back from telling his father. Even knowing how pleased he would be did not prompt Cory to share that good news. Obviously, they were both evading the subject for different reasons and Cory wasn't even sure what his reason was.

The next two days were spent tramping in the woods from one end of the property to the other, searching for the stakes that marked the boundaries. The Town Chairman had assured Michael that the properties had been surveyed and marked only a year or so ago. With relief, Cory realized that his father had not seen a plat book to learn that Annie Winters had property just six miles away. Surely, if he continued to stay at the cabin, his father would learn somewhere or somehow that his own mother lived only a few miles away. Several times Cory had entertained the idea of going home to protect Annie's secret, and yet, he wanted to have time to solve this awful injustice.

Planning ahead, Cory and his dad had brought swim suits for a quick workout at the lake after their investigation of the southern boundary of their property. Coming from the south, they began to circle the lake when Michael discovered large cat prints in the saturated soil on the east shore. Following the prints, it was clear that the huge cat had come for water in several places along the whole east half of the lake from Jenny's side to Cory's.

"Look!" his dad said pointing to a very large and very fresh set of prints just a few feet from their dock. Setting his fist into the print as a means of measuring it, he looked up at Cory with concern in his eyes. "I know that you're worried about Jenny coming to the lake alone, Cory, but keep in mind that you, too, are at risk with a cat this size."

While they swam, Cory thought about the cat. He was glad that Mr. Wharton had stopped Jenny from coming to the lake, despite the fact that she was so angry with him. Strange, how he missed seeing her.

Chapter 8

A series of crisp, cool days followed a severe storm that demolished the shower, damaged the water-wheel, and tore a large piece of roof off the shed, providing a long list of repair jobs that kept Cory and his dad busy until the hot and humid days returned. Working side by side and accomplishing their tasks in half the time it took to build everything in the first place, brought Cory a great sense of satisfaction. He and his father were now the same height and much the same weight. Except for the color of their eyes, one was the image of the other, and the work of each day brought them closer together, bonding them as friends as well as family. They laughed at their errors, since neither of them professed to be a carpenter, and argued over the right way to do things, but the serious subjects of football and music were never topics of conversation to ruin things.

After chores on the first evening of the returning hot, humid days, father and son chased along the trail to the lake with a small cooler of sodas, and a pail filled with sandwiches and fruit. Although it took nearly twenty minutes to run to the lake, Cory waited until they was almost halfway there before admitting he had to go back.

"I forgot something," he hollered at the figure in front of him as they jogged along the path.

His dad stopped and turned. "Whatever it is, we don't need it," he shouted back.

" I'll only be a few minutes," Cory explained, as he turned and started back along the trail. "You continue on."

It had suddenly struck him that it was time to stop hiding behind his excuses. Tonight he would play his guitar at the lake for his father and take the laughter, verbal abuse, or whatever argument resulted from it. If he couldn't handle that, then he really was a whimp. No matter what response he received from his father, Cory also intended to tell him that he would play football his senior year. Since he had already made the choice, Cory refused to let the anger or frustration that he might feel this evening to change his mind.

When he reached the dock with his guitar, he merely hung it from a tree and joined his dad already boldly stroking toward the opposite shore. The surface water of the lake was close to the highest temperature that it would reach this summer and only a deep dive hinted at its spring-fed nature. Because the nights were beginning to cool more quickly after sunset each evening, the lake temperature would soon start its seasonal decline.

As they sat on the dock with their legs dangling over the edge, they hungrily consumed their sandwiches and fruit while discussing the possibility of catching any of the fish that could be seen occasionally in the deep areas. Neither of them knew what kind they were or whether they were edible, but Michael suggested that they get a small boat and the proper gear when they returned next year. Cory looked at his dad in surprise.

"You mean you would consider coming back next year?" he said in amazement.

His father nodded.

"Here, at the cabin?"

Again, the nod.

This was turning into one great summer! With a huge grin on his face, Cory left the dock to retrieve his guitar. Without a word he sat down next to his dad and began playing a tune so popular that it would be impossible not to recognize it. As the melody floated through the air, Cory watched his father from of the corner of his eye, expecting… What was he expecting? Could his father hate ALL music, or just classical? Was football so important, there was nothing else? The questions that flew through his mind were eventually drowned out by the beautiful music that resonated through the warm and humid evening air.

With difficulty, Cory tried to clear his mind and concentrate only on his playing, moving from familiar songs to instrumental music and finally to the most familiar of the classical pieces. Regardless of his father's comments, Cory would never totally give up playing the guitar. He might have to put it aside for awhile, but nothing could keep him from going back to it, because with it, came happiness. It was impossible for him to play without smiling, and he moved from one piece of music to another without pausing. Finally he let the notes melt away and he stopped playing.

Cory stared at the lake, not trusting himself to look at his dad. They sat in absolute silence until the smile faded from Cory's face and his mind began to jump from one assumption to another. He was about to stand up and gather their things to leave when his father finally spoke.

"It's time to go if we want to reach the cabin before it's too dark to see." That was all he said.

In silence they walked back to the cabin.

His father was in the habit of reading at the end of each day and after lighting a few candles, Cory propped his book open and pretended to join him, while the pressure of the silence hung over him. It was only the knowledge that his father was inclined to weigh all aspects of a problem before making a decision, that conquered Cory's impulse to question him. When his dad was ready to talk about it, he would bring up the subject of his guitar and they would hopefully discuss things without an argument. Coming to that conclusion, Cory finally put down his book and climbed the ladder to the loft. Sleep, however, was hard to achieve until well after two o'clock and then nightmares of stalking a cougar filled the remainder of his night.

Another sultry, August day greeted them in the morning. Cory made plans to gather firewood for the following winter while his father drove to Woodville to complete some business and purchase supplies. Since the prospect of using the cabin for weekend getaways, as it was intended, had been discussed at length that morning, they agreed to begin building a cache of firewood for the coming winter. It was clear that the cabin was no longer a place of unhappy memories. As time passed, new memories were being built and the old ones washed away, leaving a fresh and cheerful atmosphere.

It wasn't just his dad's attitude that said he was enjoying the days at the cabin, it was the constant grin that surfaced as they did things together in both work and play. Although a hesitation appeared when Cory introduced the guns, his father quickly got into the spirit of competition, trying his best and failing to outshoot his son. When his father could stop laughing long enough to appreciate Cory's sapling catapult for throwing items to shoot, he still lost.

Now, with the thought of preparing the place for winter, they had rigged a litter, like those of the Indians in the old west, and Cory was just setting out to gather firewood, when a four-wheeler came down the path from the logging road. It was Jenny.

Thinking quickly, Cory went to meet her as she entered the clearing. Stepping in front, forced her to stop the machine and turn off the engine, as he hurriedly warned her not to mention Annie when she met his dad. She followed him back to the cabin where introductions were made.

"Dad, I'd like you to meet Jenny Wharton. Jenny, this is my dad, Michael Redlam," Cory said, staring meaningfully at her.

She reached out to shake hands and only a slight flare of her eyes registered her surprise when she saw the beautiful, strikingly blue features that looked back at her. "Hi," she said, timidly. "I'm glad to meet you."

"Glad to meet you, too, Jenny, and I apologize for rushing off, but I have a schedule that must be met," he explained as he slid into the Jeep. "I should be back by five, Cory."

The Jeep bumped over the uneven ground and was absorbed into the foliage of the trees as it struggled down the primitive road.

Swinging to face Cory, she blurted, "Your dad looks like Annie! What's that all about?"

"What did you come here for?" he asked, evading her question.

Jenny explained her arrival in a rapid flow of words.

"Dad sends his apologies, but the big game is going to be on Friday rather than Thursday as originally planned. He really hopes you'll still be able to play. I'm afraid he's pinned all his hopes on you and Pooter. For a week after your practice, all he could talk about was his 'team' and he wasn't talking about the eleven guys—he meant the team of you and Pooter. Now tell me about your father."

"I can't tell you anything," Cory said as he began picking up the ropes of the litter.

With her hands on her hips she glared at him and blocked his way.

"Look, I think my dad and Annie might be related, but I promised her that I would not tell anyone, especially my dad."

"That makes absolutely no sense," Jenny complained.

In frustration, Cory dropped the ropes and pulled Jenny to a chair on the porch where he told her the whole story after receiving a multitude of promises that she would keep the information to herself.

"Now, do you understand why Annie doesn't want my dad to know that she's here?"

She nodded. "It is so sad and unfair, but still wonderful, because she might be your grandmother! What are you going to do about it, Cory?"

"I'll figure something out, but right now, I need to get firewood and you need to go home."

" I came over for another reason," Jenny started to say, then paused. "Look, I'm sorry for getting angry with you…again," she said meaningfully. "But you can't imagine the teasing I've taken because of your warning. The boys are relentless. Now that I have to stay out of the woods, it's hard to get away from them, even for a moment of peace." Her smile softened her complaint.

"I'm sorry they tease you," Cory said, "but the cougar danger is very real. Don't your brothers care about protecting you, Jenny? My dad and I have seen the tracks and there are many of them all around the lake. Big ones!"

"Of course they want to protect me, but they don't believe the prints are real. This is just the kind of trick they would play on me by placing…cat prints…all over the…ground. Wait a minute! That really IS the kind of trick they would play."

"Jenny. Before you jump to any false conclusion, this should be checked out. Dad and I think the prints are real and they're fresh. Look, don't do anything foolish. I have to leave, so get your four-wheeler and go home." With that, Cory picked up the ropes of the litter and started walking toward the northwest.

"Wait!" Jenny shouted. "I'll go with you. No one expects me back until dinner and I desperately need a day without my brothers."

Cory frowned but understood and, after a moment's hesitation, he simply handed her one of the ropes to pull the litter. With axes secured to the frame, they began dragging it to the area near Cory's favorite raspberry clearing about an hour's trek away.

With the many storms that had rolled through the area this summer, the numbers of downed trees were many and it did not take long to cut the fallen trees into small chunks and split each chunk into the right-sized pieces of firewood. Stacked and tied to the litter, the wood weighed more than one of them could have pulled and Jenny grinned when they discovered that Cory needed her help. After attaching short lengths of rope to form harnesses, the litter moved smoothly with the combined efforts of both of them. They had swung the litter around to face their homeward direction before filling it, and they were carefully readjusting the ropes when Cory smelled trouble.

A small clearing, no more than an acre in size, filled with brambles of both raspberry and blackberry canes, lay between them and their route to the cabin, and at the edge of that clearing stood a huge black bear that stared alarmingly at them. Jenny was standing directly in front of Cory, and before she had a moment to react, he wrapped his left arm around her waist and smothered her cry with his right hand, smoothly pulling her to him and quickly whispering in her ear, "Don't scream! Don't run!"

Slowly Cory moved to the side of Jenny and only withdrew his hand from her mouth when she nodded ever so slightly to let him know that she would not scream. "Drop your arms, don't look at the bear, don't move," he ordered in a whisper.

The huge bear had risen on her hind legs, sniffing the air with a swing of her head from side to side. She released a low gutteral sound as she lowered her massive body to the ground and moved a few steps closer to them. Once more she rose on her hind legs, increasing her fearful size in an act of intimidation. The half-grunt, half-growl issued from deep in her throat and again, she moved closer to Jenny and Cory. The odor of bear was almost as frightening as her nearness. She was now just inches away from them.

With his left arm still around Jenny's waist, Cory felt her tremble when the bear finally put her nose against his shirt and sniffed audibly. Slowly the mammoth head lowered to Cory's right hand where the familiar rough tongue flicked over his fingers. It was at that moment that Cory knew this was the mother bear he had encountered before. He let his eyes sweep the woods until he spotted her cub high in the branches of an oak tree. Moving slowly around them, the bear licked and smelled first Cory, then Jenny until, apparently satisfied with the situation, she turned and ambled off to retrieve her cub.

Motionless, Jenny and Cory watched her slow progress away from them through the tall grass and tangled brush, stopping only once to swing her impressive head around to stare at them. Then, in a casual manner, she shifted her attention to the cub and strolled off in its direction.

Until the cub descended from the tree and ran after its mother, Cory and Jenny never moved. Then a sound, somewhere between a sob and a moan, came from Jenny's lips as she wrapped her arms around Cory and buried her face against him. She was shaking and he simply held her until she was calm. Finally she sat down on the firewood. Watching her intently, Cory crouched in front of her.

"Are you okay, Jenny?" he asked with clear concern in his voice.

Unable to speak, she simply nodded, but her eyes betrayed how frightened she had been. Helping her to her feet, he handed one of the ropes to her and in silence they pulled the litter back to the cabin.

By the time they managed to drag their heavy load into the yard and over to the crib for storage, Jenny was worrying about another problem and after repeated promises from Cory, he assured her that he had no intention of telling her brothers that she had been frightened by the bear. When he couldn't understand why that was a problem, Jenny attempted to clarify once more what life was like with her brothers.

"My brothers are really terrific guys and I love them," Jenny repeated, "but they get so caught up in teasing and they take cowardice as a serious flaw in people. It won't just be teasing that will be hard to take. It will be their scorn for anyone who is frightened easily, and that will be me!"

Cory was beginning to feel angry. What type of brothers put that kind of pressure on their sister who was brave enough to let a wild bear lick her hand? Imagine what they would say if they knew he played the guitar, and worse yet—classical music.

"You never screamed and didn't run or faint!" he stated sharply. "You faced a bear and even let it lick you! How many times have your brothers had THAT experience?"

"Everything will be fine, if you don't tell them about this," Jenny stated with a questioning look.

They were sitting on the porch drinking lemonade from a package mix in an attempt to cool down after their strenuous work.

Finally Cory gave in and laughed. "I promise, I

promise, I promise!" he said. Then, in a more serious tone, he reminded her of the promise she had made to keep the secret about Annie until Cory could figure out a way to bring his father and grandmother together peacefully. After one more promise from Cory, Jenny mounted the four-wheeler and headed for home.

Most of the wood was stacked in the covered crib that he and his father had built along the north side of the shed when the sound of the Jeep could be heard on the logging road, and as Cory threw the last pieces of firewood onto the stack, the Jeep crept into the clearing.

While Cory helped his dad unload the vehicle and put the supplies away, he sensed that something was troubling his father. He seemed unusually quiet throughout the preparation of dinner and into the evening. Except for the answers to direct questions, they ate in silence and little was said until they sat on the porch at sunset

When his father suddenly tossed the paper he was reading onto the floor and sat back in the rocker, Cory knew a discussion was coming. He could think of nothing that he had done wrong, but the sensation that he was in trouble would not leave him. He put aside the knife he had been using to cut a piece of leather into strips to be used as bindings, and sat back to watch his dad. Suddenly, it struck Cory that his dad looked tired and for the first time, looked his age of forty-one.

"I met a very interesting gentleman in Woodville today," his father began. "I stated my name for the Postmaster in order to get some business documents that I hope can be sent to me, and the fellow behind me, asked if I was related to a Cory Redlam. I asked him how he knew you. Turns out that he is Jenny's father, Bill Wharton."

Until this moment, Cory had no idea what this was

all about. Now he knew. It was about football! Father and son stared at each other while Cory waited for the rest.

"Cory, why didn't you tell me about this football game you agreed to play?"

"Dad, it really isn't an important game. It's just a bet that Mr. Wharton and the coach made to see who can come up with the best team. Some of the guys have been out of high school for a couple of years and some are only freshmen. I guess it's more of a contest than anything. And I agreed to play only because Jenny's brother, Pooter, made me mad."

A frown crossed his father's face and Cory hurried to defend his words.

"I know! I know! Never make a decision when you're mad. You told me that a hundred times. But you can't imagine how maddening the Wharton boys can be!"

Cory shifted his legs and exhaled loudly. "What I should have told you the day you arrived, Dad, was that I had made my choice to play on the football team my senior year, if the coach will still want me."

His father leaned forward. "With your skills, Cory, the coach would be insane not to want you, but let me ask you an important question. Were you angry when you made that decision?"

"No," Cory admitted, shaking his head.

The grin that swept across his father's face told Cory more than the congratulations and compliments that his father repeatedly voiced. They sat on the porch talking about his dad's favorite subject until long after sunset, and both of them went to bed exhausted. It had been a very full day.

Chapter 9

Sliding further under the blankets and curling his body into a ball did not change the draft of cold air that flowed from the open window near his head. When Cory's senses were finally awake enough, he slid one arm from under the bedding and, reaching over his head, he pulled the window shut. Sounds from beneath the loft, along with fragrances of coffee and frying bacon rose from the kitchen. In the stupor of waking, it took a moment for it to register that his dad rarely got up before he did.

It took a few more minutes for him to shake himself fully awake and slip into his clothes. As he stepped off the ladder and into the kitchen, he noticed that a duffle-bag was packed and sitting on the floor by the door.

"Morning," Cory said. "What gives?" He pointed to the duffle as his father looked up from the sizzling bacon.

His dad had a sheet pan filled with bread, ready to pop into the stove, and a carton of eggs sitting next to the bacon. The table was set and two mugs of coffee had been poured. While he lifted the curled strips of bacon from the grease, he finally responded.

"Good morning. Did you sleep well?"

Cory watched his dad, but did not answer. Two could play this game. Instead, he sat down at the table and took a sip of the hot coffee. His dad was leaving, obviously, or maybe he was going to send Cory home. Wait! That really wasn't home. Home was here!

The longer the silence, the wilder his thoughts, and the shorter his patience. By the time the eggs, bacon, and toast were on the table, Cory had no appetite.

"Okay, Dad, what's going on?" he demanded.

His father put down the piece of toast on which he

had been carefully spreading a small pat of butter. "I'm sorry, Cory," he said, shaking his head. "I wanted to tell you last night that I have to leave, but I just couldn't bring myself to spoil the evening. A business merger that I was handling has met some problems and I need to fly to England for a few days. Maybe a week."

The pained look on his dad's face deflated Cory's anger that had been steadily growing and told him that the need to leave was not a choice. They stared at each other.

"I've had a great time here, Cory," his father said with feeling.

"Me, too!"

Cory looked at the duffle bag. "When?" he asked.

"This noon, as soon as I can get everything organized."

"Does that mean I have to leave here, too?"

A huge grin flooded his father's face. "Not unless you want to," he said. "I've been so proud of how you've taken care of yourself, both here and at home. The cougar is a worry, but you are aware of that, and you know enough to carry one of the guns.

In the past, my work has prevented me from getting to know you, but the last two weeks…"

"Eight days, Dad!"

"Okay, eight days! Anyway, they've been great! I'd like to come back here as soon as the business is settled. With the fresh groceries that I purchased yesterday, you should be just fine until I return."

Although the food on their plates had cooled a little, their appetites never noticed it as they each devoured half the toast, eggs, and bacon.

Then the lawn was tackled with a great deal of energy, shifting the manual mower from one to the other in a contest to see who could cut the biggest patch in ten minutes. Almost everything one of them did was a challenge to the other and half the morning was gone before they knew it.

Sprawled in the chairs on the porch, Cory and his dad carefully tested the chokecherry-juice concoction that had been laboriously made the previous day. Sweat ran down their faces and soaked their clothes while they argued over who cut the most lawn in the shortest amount of time. During the contest, there had been some crazy, funny moments which they rehashed now, causing them to laugh all over again.

The simple movement of checking a watch, however, sobered both of them and the laughter ended in silence. Cory's thoughts went to Annie and the dilemma he faced in getting his dad and grandmother together. He feared the opportunity was slipping away from him. Will his dad really be back in a week? School would be starting in three weeks. Was that enough time? He HAD to get his dad to talk about his parents. Without being fully conscious of it, he had risen from the chair and was pacing back and forth on the porch with his hands jammed in his pockets when he finally spoke.

"Dad?" Cory began. "Did you love your dad as much as I love you?"

His father smiled. "I don't know, son. How much is that?"

"Big Bucks, Dad! Big Bucks!"

Cory answered automatically in the same way he had said those very words when he was small and then they both laughed because it brought back happy memories.

"Seriously, Dad," he continued. "I need to know about my grandparents."

When his question met only silence, the frustration Cory felt slowly shifted to anger. "Don't you think I have a right to know about my own family?" he demanded.

"They're DEAD, Cory!"

"That's all the more reason I should know EVERYTHING about them, since I'll never meet them," Cory argued. "Dad, I need to know who I am, and it's important to me to know that I had more family than just the two of us."

"Cory! You knew your mother!"

"Yes! Until I was FIVE! How much do you think I can remember of her when we NEVER talk about her?"

The words rushed out of his mouth as though they had been there under pressure and he plopped into the chair, frustrated and angered by his outburst.

Michael Redlam set his glass on the floor and leaned forward in his chair. Concern was etched on his face and the piercing blue eyes seemed to look into Cory's mind.

"All right, Cory," he said slowly. "What do you want to know?"

"Everything!" Cory said hurriedly. "First, describe your parents."

The description of his grandfather left an ache in Cory's stomach as he felt the loss of never being able to meet him, but it helped him to understand the agony that Annie had lived with over so many years.

For several minutes Michael explained how his dad had taught him about all the different sports and trained him in each of them just as HE had done with Cory. His love for his father was evident in everything he said about him.

Although there was a huge difference in their ages, it was clear that Michael had loved his sister, Amanda, too, and had been the protective older brother. But when Michael's mother was described, Cory steeled his outward expression from displaying the happiness that swept through him. Except for the style and color of her hair, Annie had not changed and without any further doubt;

she was his grandmother!

"If they're all dead, they must have died young, especially your sister," Cory prompted.

As though exhausted, his father slumped against the back of the chair and shifted his gaze to the sky and then off into the distance with an obvious struggle to control his emotions. He stood up and started pacing the floor of the porch. Cory waited patiently and finally his father began to repeat the terrible story of the car accident. To his surprise, it matched Annie's completely, including her insistence that something had been wrong with the brakes.

At the far end of the porch his dad stopped his pacing and stood there with his hands in his pockets. "Life is all about making choices, Cory." He seemed to be staring into the distance at nothing. Then he swung around and their eyes met. "Sometimes we make foolish choices and we pay dearly for them."

When he returned to his chair and slumped into it, he sighed deeply. "I blamed my mother for the death of my dad and sister," he admitted unhappily. "I was seventeen and thought I knew everything. I was so angry that this had happened and I took it out on her instead of being the son my father would have wanted me to be. It is a shameful part of my life, Cory, and I never want you EVER to treat another human being as I treated my mother. I attended the funerals and left home…never to return. I wouldn't even speak to her."

"You hated her?" Cory asked.

"Yes!"

"But you don't hate her now, do you?"

"Of course not, but it's too late! When I went back eight years later, the neighbors told me that she had died, and I have lived with the regret ever since that I had not been loving enough to forgive her for the accident."

The misery in his father's eyes matched the misery he had seen in Annie's and at the moment, Cory was struggling to keep her secret as he had promised. It was clear that his dad had forgiven his mother long ago and that he still loved her very much. This news brought a fresh surge of happiness and excitement through Cory's body and he had to fight the urge to tell his dad about Annie.

When they packed his father's briefcase and duffle bag into the Jeep at noon and said goodbye, Cory felt a conflict of emotions. On the one hand he didn't want his father to leave, but his leaving gave Cory the opportunity to see Annie and tell her the good news. However, it was too late to start out for her place today, and he had to quiet his enthusiasm and be content with the prospect of seeing her tomorrow.

Returning to the porch as his father drove away, Cory collected his guitar from its familiar place in the summer kitchen and sat outside playing it for over an hour. Since that night at the lake when he had first played for his father, Cory had not taken his guitar to the lake again. Although he had resolved to accept his father's silence on the subject, he was not ready to give up his playing and every evening since that night, Cory took out the guitar and played it on the porch with his father silently reading while music flowed around him. Now that his father was aware of the guitar, his silence was more confusing than ever. It had been easier to understand when they simply argued about his playing, when his father only knew about his desire rather than his ability. Was his playing worse than he thought? Cory was aware that he had much to learn, but his instructor had repeatedly complimented him on the quickness with which he learned and the quality of his playing. Was that a lie? The negative result of his father's silence on the subject was the destruction of Cory's confidence in his playing. Then again, he constantly reminded himself that his dad was a man who looked at every bit of evidence before drawing a conclusion and making a statement. Cory would wait!

During the night, the temperature dropped below freezing and the morning brought frost and a thin layer of ice on the water in Cory's copper tub for the first time since the spring. Fall was coming. It was already evident in the slight change in the sound of the leaves when they brushed against each other, altering the muffled sound in summer to the raspy, dry sound of autumn. Too fast! The seasons were changing too fast and there were so many things that needed to be decided, changed, or settled before he went home.

The thought of leaving here and going back to attend school brought no joy. Cory had a few select friends that he had missed over the summer, but too many of his classmates simply harassed him about football and teased him about being afraid of getting roughed-up in the tough sport. Only his closest friends knew anything about his guitar playing and their loyalty was enough to prevent them from teasing. Although his build was athletic and his features attractive, most of the girls went steady with the guys who were active in sports and they considered him strange to have the ability and yet not want to be a part of the team.

Despite the arguments, fights, and dislike that stood between him and the Wharton brothers, Cory felt a strange respect for them and he liked them as a family. His feelings for Jenny confused him. One minute he was angry with her, then he felt sorry for her, then he wanted to protect her, then, the next moment, he just wanted to be with her. She kept popping into his thoughts at all times of the day, and there was something missing if he hadn't seen her for a long time. All these thoughts ran through his mind as he jogged on the trail through the woods in the chill of the early morning.

When he reached Annie's, he ran across the lawn in time to sweep her off the steps as she came down, and swing her around in a circle with her feet off the ground. By the time he put her down, she was laughing so hard, she staggered, and Cory had to catch her before she fell.

"Cory!" she cried. "What has gotten into you?"

"Grandmother," he said, meaningfully, "I have to talk to you."

The blue eyes widened and stared at him. "I love the sound of that, but are you sure I'm your grandmother, Cory?"

He took her hand and led her to the chairs on the porch where they sat for half an hour while he explained what his dad had said yesterday before leaving. Cory reassured her that he had kept his promise not to tell his dad about her.

"He'll be gone only a week," Cory explained. "If I know my dad, nothing will prevent him from watching me play football at the Wharton's the following week." Cory paused and then added, "I want you to be at that game, Annie."

She started to shake her head, but he hurried to explain.

"Mr. Wharton and Coach Larson make a big deal of this football competition. From what Jenny told me, all the neighbors and students from Woodville High School, including parents, show up for a whole day of football, food, and dancing. They make a huge party of the contest. You're invited, too." He looked at her pleadingly.

"I know about their game, Cory. I've been invited before, but you don't understand." Annie frowned. "What if you're wrong about your father's change of heart? What if he still hates me?"

"So, what have you got to lose?" Cory asked boldly.

"YOU!" she responded immediately. "I can't handle even the thought of Michael taking you away from me." Tears pooled in her eyes. "But, I so want to see him," she murmured. "It has been twenty-four years since he left home."

Cory took her hands in his and looked at the sad but beautiful face. "Do you trust me?" he asked. She nodded. "Then trust me now!" he replied firmly. She smiled and then, slowly nodded again.

Was it possible to actually feel physically lighter when one was happy? And why did the air smell cleaner, the sky look bluer, and the ground feel softer as Cory traveled back to the cabin that day? The last remnants of blueberries that he scooped from the low growing bushes that he passed on his way tasted even sweeter than the ones he had picked a week ago.

Late that afternoon, while he worked on the raft that he and his father had started to build for the lake, Jenny called to ask if Cory could come for another football practice tomorrow. Recovering from the surprise of receiving a call from her, he told her about his conversation with his dad and then with Annie. Jenny found it exciting to think that a sad story had a chance for a happy ending and was thrilled with the thought that Annie might finally attend one of their football celebrations. She offered to have someone in her family get Annie on that day. They both agreed that it should be a surprise for his dad.

August heat reached into the sweltering nineties on Wednesday when Cory arrived at the Wharton home. As usual, the frenzy of activity surrounding the family complex made Cory smile. Gobb and Truck were attempting to corner a small, black and white goat in a paddock on the side of the barn. Jenny was scattering feed for the chickens and several geese, while Coonsey, Pooter, and Chunk were repairing old, wooden bleachers to be hauled into the field for the game next week.

Heavy farm equipment sat near the field, having harvested the final crop of alfalfa for the season. Now that the hay was cut, dried, and baled, the field, though rough, would serve as their football grid. From Jenny's explanation, Coach Larson would actually have the field marked like they did for their regular high school games.

Today was more than practice. Although Mr. Wharton viewed Cory as his "secret weapon" and had not wanted to reveal his ability, Coach Larson had asked for a scrimmage and could not be refused. They would also receive whatever jerseys and helmits that might fit them from the school's supply of old, unused equipment.

Cory sat on the porch steps watching the activity and enjoying the theatrical performance of Truck and Gobb with the little goat who continued to evade their grasp, when Mrs. Wharton joined him. They both found the tableau in front of them amusing.

"I know the boys can appear to be a little mean-spirited at times," she said in an apologetic tone, "but they are more often very loving sons."

Cory looked at her and wondered what point she was trying to make. He wasn't sure whether she was warning him or apologizing to him. Without another word she got up and went back into the house, leaving him more confused. Jenny was just about to join him when Pooter came over.

"Can I talk to you a minute?" he asked, motioning for Cory to follow him. They walked a short distance from all the activity before he continued. "Just thought I'd warn you. My brothers think you ratted on us about the dock, since my mother has demanded that they build another one. Without stealing this time," he added. "She's given us two days to have it done. To say that they are angry would be an understatement."

"Why would they think that I told her?" Cory asked.

"Because she always says, 'a little bird told me', and that's a dead giveaway that some busybody tattled on us."

"Jenny?"

"NEVER!"

"Why aren't YOU angry?" Cory asked suspiciously.

Pooter stood with his hands jammed in his pockets, appearing to search Cory's face for the truth. "I don't really know, except, for some strange reason, I don't think you would do that."

"I didn't."

"Well, just be on your guard." With that, Pooter walked away.

When the scrimmage began, Cory was surprised to learn that Coach Larson's team was composed of the entire high school varsity with the exception of Pooter who could hardly refuse to play on his father's team. Although the game went well and Cory continued to impress those who watched him play, he was conscious of his luck to be on the Wharton team playing WITH the brothers instead of against them. Whenever he was close enough for an unnoticed elbow or a well-placed knee, he knew that Pooter's warning had been totally underrated.

The scrimmage was stopped at a tied score and both teams left the field mentally prepared to win the real game next week. After briefings by each coach during a cool-down period, refreshments were served and friendly conversations flowed.

While Jenny went to fetch more sodas for herself and Cory, Gobb sat down next to him on the lawn and, in his intimidating way, casually said, "Well, Whimp, you've done it now. If we catch you in the woods, you're dead meat!" Then with a false smile, he gave Cory a pseudo-friendly small shove and stood up to walk away.

"Trouble?" Jenny questioned as she handed Cory a soda.

"Not for me," he reassured her.

"Cory, you're always concerned about my safety, but what about yours? I'm not saying that I believe in your cougar, but since YOU believe in it, isn't YOUR life in danger?"

Cory laughed. "You are absolutely right." he said. "That's why I always carry that large hunting knife that your brothers are constantly teasing me about. Don't worry, Jenny. I promised my dad that I would be extra careful while he's gone."

When Coach Larson called for his team and the others who had traveled to the practice with him to load into the borrowed school bus, and those who had come by car left, Jenny walked with Cory to the edge of the woods.

"Please be careful, Cory."

"I will," he promised, sliding his arms into the straps of his backpack, thinking that the Wharton boys were much more of a threat than any old cougar.

He had not gone far on the trail when he reconsidered the fact that the hunting knife was in the pack and not at his waist. A lot of good it would do there, he thought and he quickly slipped the leather sheath onto his belt.

The threat from Gobb worried him. The more he got to know Jenny and her parents, the more he wanted to repair the disagreements and hatred that her brothers felt for him. However, at the moment, that all seemed to be going downhill. How could the parents be so nice and the sons such morons?

All Cory could think of as he played his guitar that evening was the relief he felt knowing that Jenny's brothers would never hear him play and would never have the opportunity to tease him about it.

Chapter 10

Early the next morning, Cory intended to continue the chore of tapping pine trees to gather pitch for their raft while he planned his approach to the problem of the Wharton boys. Schemes to mend the rift with Gobb and his brothers had been forming and dissolving in his thoughts, one after the other, until Cory felt his mind would explode from the effort. But nothing felt workable. The situation seemed so bad now that it certainly couldn't get any worse. Or, could it?

From the time he arrived at the cabin in the beginning of June, Cory had never locked the doors. He could see very little reason for doing so, and Annie's frequent gifts of supplies confirmed the practicality of leaving things open as they were today. There wasn't much to steal and no one around to take anything, so without a second thought, he packed his gear and took off for the pine plantings.

Gathering pitch from the trees consumed an extreme amount of time when valued against the quantity of product collected, and only someone with a great deal of patience would attempt it. Certain areas of the forest had been replanted twenty years ago with pine trees which now stood in perfect rows of absolutely straight, limbless poles, topped with a short display of needled branches. The sap was thick and difficult to collect but could be used to waterproof wood in order to get it to float.

Returning now with his precious, but minute, supply of pine pitch, Cory noticed several sets of fresh human footprints in the soft sand along the creek near his path and wondered who could possibly be at his cabin. Other than Jenny, his dad, and Annie, no one had ever come to his property.

Hurrying to the door where sounds from within could be heard, he swung it open ready to welcome or challenge his guests, when he jerked to a stop. Apparently his guests only came to bring him a present and there it was! On the table, eating the last of his bread was a huge skunk, who, at the sound of Cory's entry, immediately swung his body around in a defensive gesture.

Backing slowly out of the cabin, Cory's thoughts churned with indecision. What should he do? How was he going to get the skunk out of his home? Once he reached the porch steps, he accepted the only weak plan he could think of, turned and ran to the creek where he quickly caught three crayfish from the shallow waters, and scrambled back to the cabin. There, he carefully and quietly placed them in plain sight on the floor of the porch about two feet in front of the open door.

Stepping back to wait patiently for the skunk to notice the food and move out of the cabin to get it, Cory remembered Gobb. The footprints at the creek were surely his and those of at least one brother. This revenge for something he didn't do was going too far. Wasn't it time for the boys to grow up? Pooter was the only one still in high school, and Cory was convinced that he would not have been a part of this. Shouldn't the older boys be acting like men instead of little kids pulling pranks like spoiled brats?

As Cory waited for the skunk to react to his live bait, he vowed he would not lower himself to their level by retaliating. Although angry now, he was determined to make peace with Gobb and his brothers. Cory could sense from yesterday that Pooter was not yet entirely on his side, but the gap was closing and he felt sure that someday they would be friends. During the football scrimmage, he and Pooter had played like a smooth-running machine, so in sync with each other that Pooter seemed to automatically know where Cory intended to throw the ball and, in turn, Cory threw it where he seemed to know Pooter would be. Now, as Cory stood on the lawn out of sight of the skunk, his patience was disappearing as all these thoughts ran through his head.

Despite the enticing food near the door, the skunk was in no hurry. Curiosity had taken over and compelled it to examine several areas of the kitchen before slowly arriving at the entrance to the cabin. By now the crayfish had separated and were several feet apart, but the skunk promptly captured and ate each one.

Meanwhile, Cory had pried open the kitchen window and forced his body through the small opening in an attempt to close the cabin door from the inside in case the skunk decided to go back in.

Surprised by the click of the closing door, the skunk raised its tail and sprayed the closest enemy—the porch rocker! Too late to save anything outside, Cory remained in the cabin until the skunk was on the lawn before he grabbed the rifle and shot it. Despite his feelings about killing animals, this one, having tasted Cory's food, would be back for more and that was not acceptable. With the shot, one more spray was released, filling the whole area with the terrible, pungent smell of skunk.

Cleaning up the mess proved to be an exercise in futility. Although Cory had washed the rocker with hot soapy water three times and dried it in the sun, it now sat about forty feet from the cabin where it still reeked. Marking the area of the lawn which had been last sprayed by the skunk, he disposed of his soapy water on top of it, hoping to dilute and bury the smell as the water soaked into the ground. Giving up, he simply avoided walking through that part of the lawn and hoped for rain and a stiff breeze to clear the disgusting odor that hung heavily in the air over everything. Thankfully the inside of the cabin had faired better and after picking up the clutter of chewed bread and washing the table, things looked somewhat normal.

Muddy footprints found on the porch confirmed Cory's conviction that Gobb was responsible for the skunk, but he would never be able to prove it, and what would it gain him even if he could? Gobb would simply deny it, and exposing his mean trick only made Cory guilty of Gobb's accusation that he had ratted on them to his mother.

To escape the intensity of the stench, Cory sat on the tiny platform at the creek that served as his "fishing dock" and wondered what to do. After a great deal of thought, he decided he would tell NO ONE about the skunk. Mrs. Wharton couldn't possibly learn about it unless Cory told someone or the culprits admitted their guilt, and when nothing happened following this incident, Gobb would realize that Cory wasn't looking for revenge and probably hadn't complained about their stealing his dock.

The more he thought about it, the more interesting his plan of silence became. Gobb would expect anger and retaliation. When he received nothing, he would be confused and more on his guard than ever, looking over his shoulder at all times, waiting for the big attack. Cory smiled. Silence might be a powerful weapon and it wouldn't hurt to let Gobb stew for awhile.

With absolutely no reason to stay at the smelly cabin, Cory took off for the lake in the middle of the afternoon where he found Jenny already lying in the sun on HIS dock watching the construction of HERS on the other side of the lake. She was stretched out in her familiar green bathing suit with wet hair in a pony tail dripping water on her shoulders. Her chin was cupped in her crossed arms and for a moment Cory thought she might be sleeping.

It was a perfect summer day—blue sky, warm but not sticky breezes and the occasional falling leaf to remind them of the coming autumn. He descended the small hill quietly and spoke only when he reached the dock.

"Mademoiselle," he inquired, "have you paid the rent for your space on this dock?"

Unaware that someone had approached from behind her, she turned with a jerk, then smiled. "Monsieur," she said in an imitation of a deep voice, "I have no need to pay rent. I am a member of the Surrette' and I am investigating the building of a dock." She ended in laughter, but as he bent down to stretch out on the logs, her reaction startled him back to reality.

"Ewww! Cory, what have you been into? You…"

"Shhh!" he whispered quickly, realizing that she could smell skunk. "Please, Jenny, don't say another word until I'm back on the dock. I don't want your brothers to hear." With that he dove smoothly into the water and while submerged he rubbed his hair and body to dislodge the smell that clung to him. Although he had soaped and washed himself with the hottest water he could stand several times last evening, the simple act of walking across the lawn seemed to reattached the odor to him.

Once more he attempted to stretch out in the sun. "Is it better?" he asked in a barely audible voice.

Cory didn't need to see the slight shake of her head. The expression on her face told him that the dip in the lake was another waste of effort. Would he smell like this forever?

"Tomato juice," Jenny whispered.

Cory had to lean toward her to hear. "Huh?"

"You use tomato juice to get rid of the smell," she explained, grinning because of the disbelieving look on his face, especially after she told him to wash his hair and bathe in it. But her confidence in its magical powers swayed his opinion to give it a try.

Securing a promise from Jenny was becoming a common practice, but he would not explain the skunk smell until she pledged to keep his secret. Because sound carries so much better across water, and they could frequently hear things that the Wharton boys were saying to each other on the opposite shore of the lake, Cory related the incident of the skunk in a voice barely more than a murmur. It pleased him to know that Jenny did not think her brothers' prank was the least bit funny, but it bothered him to discover that she was not surprised at the trick. Getting Gobb to accept him was going to be a bigger challenge than he had previously thought.

"I want to make peace with your brothers," he said.

" Right now, they're too mad for that to happen," Jenny admitted. "Actually, they blame both of us for the work they're doing right now. They think you ratted on them and I was a traitor by defending you, so we're both in trouble."

"Why?"

"Because they expect me to be on their side whenever…"

"No! I mean, why did you defend me?"

Jenny turned to look carefully at Cory as though expecting to find truth written on his face. "You've been honest with me even though I jumped to conclusions and said some pretty nasty things. And, you've kept my secret about the bear. I appreciate that. Then, too, Pooter seems to trust you and he only pretends to be angry with you to save himself from the unnecessary trouble with his brothers."

"I like Pooter and I'd like to be friends with him," Cory admitted.

"In that case, don't call him Pooter," Jenny suggested. "He hates the nickname, and can you blame him? He's seventeen-years-old and we still call him Pooter."

As the afternoon progressed, they alternated between swimming and watching the construction of the dock. Cory assumed that their presence at the lake did not help the attitudes of the brothers, but he enjoyed being with Jenny and would not let the opinions of her brothers stop him from seeing her.

On his return walk to the cabin, he made a mental note to remember to call Pooter by his given name of Alex. In fact, every time he thought of him from now on, he would think of him as Alex.

It was rather difficult to get to sleep that night with the damp air enhancing the smell of skunk. For that matter, eating dinner wasn't that pleasant either, but Cory refused to let it anger him. He had spent the evening as usual with his guitar while he waited for the call from his father, and then went to bed early.

During the night, a large animal destroyed his garden. When he surveyed the damages in the morning, only the presence of huge bear tracks convinced him that the Wharton boys had not done this. The stakes, that had surrounded the garden to keep the deer out, were tossed like toothpicks across the yard and vegetables had been torn from the ground and partially eaten or trampled. Upon close inspection, Cory even found smears of blood on the logs which sided the cabin. Concluding that the animal might have been wounded, Cory felt the discomfort of fear. All bears under any circumstances were a threat, but a wounded one was even more dangerous.

With the shotgun loaded and draped across his arm, he made a careful search of the entire clearing around the cabin before heading to Annie's. Near the northwest corner, where the bear had obviously come down Cory's path from her place, he discovered a smear of blood on the leaves of a raspberry cane. This was the same direction from which he had twice encountered the mother bear and her cub. Was it possibly her? He hoped not. Though it was not logical, he had grown fond of the bear and the thought of her injured, saddened him.

Cory reasoned correctly that even if this bear was normally less aggressive than most, being injured might change its behavior and he impressed upon Annie the need for her to carry a gun if she entered the woods. He trusted her to keep her promise until he found the bear and they could determine how much of a threat she really was. For now, Annie promised she would carry a weapon and be on guard.

Although he walked all the way to Annie's to warn her about the danger of an injured bear, it was not until his return along that trail, that he noticed an area of tall brush that was trampled down as though a large animal had been lying there. Further investigation suggested that something had been severely wounded in that same spot. There were several pools of dried blood. Had poachers shot the bear and only wounded it? If this was HIS bear, where was the cub? Or could that have been the reason for shooting the mother? To get the cub?

As he left the woods and stepped into the clearing near his cabin, Cory halted. There at the corner of the garden was a bulk of black fur lying on the ground. Slowly he moved forward with the shotgun ready to fire should he be forced to. When he drew nearer, he could see that the bear was alive and cautiously eating the remains of his garden, and on its left shoulder a large patch of dried blood surrounded a flow of fresh blood which glistened in the sunlight. Slowly Cory advanced in steps so hesitantly that it reminded him of a kid's game that required you to step forward without being noticed by another player.

When the bear was finally aware of Cory, it lumbered to its feet and staggered on three legs with the front left paw lifted from the ground. Disturbed by Cory's presence, it rose on hind legs, emitted a mixture of growl and moan, then lowered its massive body to a shaky stand.

During the movements, Cory spotted the strip of white fur that covered a small swath of the bear's hind foot, and he was sure that this was, indeed, his mother bear. He could only assume that the cub had been most likely killed or taken to be sold.

In a soft, soothing tone Cory began talking to the injured bear, hoping she would recognize him. Continuing the flow of assuring words, he moved a step or two closer every time she shifted her gaze. Carefully he watched the reaction of the bear with each slow step he took. Now only five or six feet stood between him and her. At this range, she would be on him before he could even bring the gun up to fire, but at the moment, he had to trust his instincts. Something about the way she looked at him suggested that she would not charge.

With the gun still cradled in his right arm he reached for the ladle in the tub on the porch and scooped out some water, taking a cautious step closer. The bear watched him with glazed eyes and lowered head. Cory moved another step closer and held out the ladle which she quickly sniffed and then proceeded to lap up until the ladle was empty. Several times she sniffed the air and leaned in his direction. Using no common sense whatsoever, but relying only on his own intuition, Cory moved closer to her and held out his hand. Her long tongue swept out of her mouth and licked his palm. As though exhausted, she slumped to the ground and lay there. Cory put the gun on the porch and brought her more water. Her wound appeared to be from a gun shot, and her actions suggested that she was perhaps feverish and in great pain.

There was nothing Cory could do for her. Surely she would not let him examine her wound, and if he did look more carefully at it, what then? He certainly could not remove the bullet or even bind the wound. Determined at least to make her as comfortable as possible, he layered dried grass in his shed as bedding, and placed a large tub of water with the remains of the vegetables, along with two small fish, on the floor next to the bedding.

Since it was already late in the day, Cory left her where she was while he went inside to fix his own dinner. Several times he checked her throughout the evening and by sunset she had moved into the shed and accepted Cory's hospitality.

Choosing the most calming pieces of music, Cory played to soothe his own mind as well as the bear's, continuing until long after dark, and then with a contented feeling he finally climbed to the loft.

Howling wolves woke him several times during the night, but the sounds were distant and although the bear was vulnerable, Cory was convinced that they were too far away to sense her weakness. Despite going to bed believing that everything would be fine in the morning, he awoke several times during the night with new concerns on his mind. Suzy, the name he assigned to the bear, was still a wild animal and an injured one at that. If he continued caring for her, she would remain a threat to anyone who came in contact with them, and contact was more likely the longer she stayed with him. By morning, common sense prevailed and Cory saw no other solution but to call the authorities and report her. Certainly, they would know what to do to help her.

However, at dawn Suzy was no longer in Cory's shed. Sometime during the night, she had wandered away after finishing the rest of the food that he had given her. With sadness, he cleaned up the bedding, noting particularly that only a small amount of blood pooled where she had been lying.

The morning air was damp and unusually warm for late in August at this northern latitude and Cory stood outside in his cut-off jeans, shirtless and barefoot, wondering where Suzy might have gone and whether she would survive. He had not been able to determine how deep or in what direction the bullet had penetrated her body. Frustrated by his inability to have helped her, he ran a hand through his thick, blond hair with its summer growth and pulled his cell phone from his pocket.

It took three calls in a half-hour to reach the correct county agency to report the bear. They promised to keep in touch after questioning him about all sorts of things that hardly seemed relevant to the problem, but Cory's most serious concern was that the bear would not be killed. He explained at length her non-aggressive behavior and received assurances that capture and treatment were their goals.

Uneasy about what course he had taken in his attempt to help Suzy, Cory tackled the accumulated chores of living at the cabin with all his pent-up energy. Bedding needed to be washed and hung on his primitive clothesline, the overflowing pile of dirty dishes on the cupboard needed to be cleaned, and the limited supply of clothing he had brought with him for the summer required a lengthy bath.

Since the feeding of the skunk and now Suzy, Cory was forced to dig into his emergency food supply for an early lunch, and while he sat at the creek eating it, Jenny called and invited him to test out her new dock this afternoon. When he questioned how she intended to get to the lake, she explained that Gobb would walk with her that far and then go off to his job of getting more firewood for the winter. On his return, he would escort her home. Satisfied that she would be safe, Cory agreed to meet her at one o'clock.

Jenny was already in the water when Cory arrived. He stood and watched the smooth and graceful swing of her arms as she swam across the lake. She was a surprisingly strong swimmer with a relaxed and easy stroke.

"Come on in!" she shouted when she saw him. "The water is the warmest it's been this summer."

After a long and energetic swim which included a race that Cory actually lost, they climbed onto the new dock and relaxed in the bright sun.

"I have a confession to make," Jenny admitted. "I'm on the swim team at school and this race was 'fixed'," she said laughingly.

Cory smiled. So ALL the Whartons are involved in sports he thought. "What else are you good at?" he asked.

"I'm not sure I'm good at any other sport, but I'm on the volleyball and baseball teams," she said in an unassuming voice.

The subject of sports was explored and dissected until Cory knew that Woodville High School was noted for its sports programs and almost every student was involved in some way. Excitedly, Jenny revealed the details of some of their most thrilling games and it was easy to see her enthusiasm as a cheerleader and spectator. He was afraid to ask about their music department in case it would put him in an uncomfortable position of explaining his own interest. The thought of Jenny's laughter or scorn for something he loved was more than he would be able to handle, so he said nothing.

Four o'clock came much too soon and as they packed up their belongings, Gobb appeared on the trail. You could see by his weary saunter that the day had not been friendly and he was not in a happy mood. He stopped about two hundred feet away and ordered Jenny to hurry and get moving. Wiping the sweat from his brow, he started turning to head for home when, from the corner of his eye, he saw the bulk of a black bear come out of the brush a short distance from Jenny.

Anticipating Gobb's instinct to protect his sister, Cory immediately ordered him to stay where he was. Then quickly he began talking slowly and gently to the bear while he moved toward Jenny in small, barely observable steps. He knew the bear was Suzy, but Gobb didn't! A knowing look and a slight nod from Cory warned Jenny. The wound on Suzy's shoulder had lost most of the dried blood which diminished the look of her injury and although the left front paw simply brushed the ground as she hobbled forward, the movement was not as shaky as yesterday.

As the bear came up to them, Cory held out his hand and Jenny followed his gesture. Continuing to speak softly, Cory waited for the rough tongue to slide over the hand he extended. Then Jenny's hand was examined. Between licks, the bear lifted her snout and sniffed the air that surrounded them. Finally satisfied with their familiar smells, she slowly staggered back into the brush the way she had come.

They stood motionless, listening to the snap of twigs and the soft rustle of branches as they sprang back into position after Suzy pushed her way through the thick growth. When they could no longer hear the bear, Gobb was still standing frozen in place with an expression of complete confusion on his face. He waited for Jenny to reach him before turning and leading her down the path toward home. He had not said one single word, not one question, no threats, no name calling, nothing!

Watching them leave, Cory smiled, knowing Jenny would never tell her brother that the bear that licked her was familiar to them. He pictured Gobb sharing the story with the other boys and the subsequent awe they would have for Jenny's bravery. Still grinning over the pleasure this situation gave him, Cory picked up his backpack and strolled toward home.

Waiting until he reached the clearing at the cabin, Cory made his second call of the day to report the new sighting of Suzy. Although he stressed the fact that the wounded bear was calm and exhibited no aggressive behavior, the authorities were convinced that they would need to capture her and move her to a more remote area or place her in a zoo. While Cory wanted to make sure she lived and that her wound healed without crippling her, he did not want her to be confined in a zoo. After a long conversation, he still had not convinced them that the best move would be the wilderness, so in resignation he simply agreed to help them capture her. Because of Cory's contact with her, they reasoned that she would remain within his area for a few days, and plans were made to attempt the rescue the following day.

To Cory's immense surprise, Suzy was back in his shed the next morning on the bed of dried grass close to a pan of fresh water that he had placed there after his call, just in case. He was feeding her the last of his garden and two fish when he heard the drone of a large pickup struggling down his path. Gently closing the door of the shed, Cory walked across his yard to meet the authorities that came for Suzy.

Struggling to fight the tears that threatened him when he tricked the mother bear into entering the bear cage that rode on a trailer behind the pickup, Cory secured a promise from the ranger in charge that she would be taken to a veterinarian and then released when she was well. Based on the ease with which she had been taken and the convictions of Cory, it appeared that she was not much of a threat.

It was a depressing day. Even the bright sunshine of an hour ago, slipped behind the clouds and refused to reappear. Cory felt miserable. The bear had trusted him.

Chapter 11

A mass of thick, dark clouds moved rapidly across the sky in the early evening, bringing night to the cabin three hours sooner than usual. When the expected call from his father came, the reception was so bad that neither one got a message from the other and Cory had to be satisfied with hearing his voice for only a few seconds.

The football game was scheduled to be played in four days and Cory had no idea if his father would be back to see it or not. For some strange reason, it mattered. He wanted his dad to be there for the game. Why? He didn't know. In fact, the game itself grew in importance, the closer they got to it. Maybe the commitment to play football his senior year was finally beginning to mean something to him.

With the sky remaining a solid sheet of gray for two days, and cold rain falling in a never-ending patter on the roof, Cory spent most of his time reading, practicing the guitar, worrying about Suzy, or reminiscing. Since there wasn't much else to do, he occupied a lot of time just thinking over the events of this wonderful summer and regretting that it would soon be over. It was fast becoming an obsession with him to become friends with the Wharton boys before he returned to school, but how to accomplish that was still a mystery.

Since Annie was never far from his thoughts, Cory wished now that he had pressured her into getting a cell phone. It was true that on days like this, he might not get through to her, but having no phone at all was a choice he wanted her to give up. She once argued that she had no family and didn't care if she died in the woods with no one to help her. But she had a family now and they cared about her. Maybe a cell phone for Christmas would be a good idea. Cory would have to work on that. It was so easy to picture Christmas here at the cabin with a fresh tree from the woods and thick snow on the ground. Common sense, however, jerked Cory back to reality and he turned his mind to the problem of the Wharton boys.

Jenny's brothers had only a week to complete the gathering of enough firewood to last their family for the entire winter. Three of the boys would be in college this year and Greg, the oldest, had plans to get married this fall after he was settled in his new job. If Cory intended to change their attitudes toward him, he needed to do something now. When the rain finally ended on Monday morning, he set out to find them, knowing that they returned to the same spot each time for the wood.

Beyond the creek, on the path to the lake, he veered off to the east following a ridge to the pine plantings. Here he took a southeasterly direction and eventually came to an area of huge boulders, remnants from the glacial period in history. Another half mile into the woods beyond that, he could hear the sound of chain saws.

While he wound his way through the woods, Cory rehearsed the words he hoped to say when he spoke to Jenny's brothers. Reasoning from Alex's hatred of his nickname, Cory concluded that the rest of the boys were probably tired of theirs too. Since he had nothing to lose, why shouldn't he call each of them by their given names? Gobb was Matt and Coonsey was Greg, but he couldn't even remember the other two. However, he could always ask Jenny and then he'd start calling them by their real names. Even if it didn't help, it certainly couldn't make things worse.

At the moment, Matt carried the anger that needed to be defused. Cory wasn't sure if the bear incident of a few days ago made any change in his attitude, but he hadn't seemed as angry when he took Jenny home that day. Certainly he had to be proud of Jenny's bravery in facing the bear.

As he closed in on the sound of the chain saws, Cory could see through the trees that only Matt and Alex were cutting wood. Hardwood trees surrounding a small abandoned gravel pit had toppled over and slid down the short embankment. They were sawing these into short logs and rolling them to a sled, where the logs would then be split and stacked for hauling.

He came up to them slowly hoping they would notice him as he approached. In a slight pause between cutting, both of them looked up at the same time to see Cory about one hundred and fifty feet away. A quick frown on Matt's face and a slight smile from Alex sent the mixed message that Cory had expected. So Matt was still his enemy. He continued striding forward as Matt bent over to gently set his chain saw down on the ground.

The next few moments passed in surrealistic slow motion while the horror of the scene in front of Cory took only seconds to register in his brain. The two brothers were standing in a forest of hardwood trees with heavy underbrush composed of small saplings and thick growth. Somewhere among the waist-high bushes a poacher's snare had been hidden. In some way, Matt had triggered it when he bent to place the chain saw on the ground.

In one swift, devastating moment, the snare caught him around the neck, jerked him off his feet, and dragged him backward and upward over the small gravel pit until his body was snapped off the ground.

Only Matt's quick reaction by grabbing the noose around the front of his neck with both hands, and the poacher's use of rope instead of wire prevented his immediate death. However, the constant and immense pressure of his knuckles against his neck would soon cut off the flow of blood to his brain and render him unconscious. He knew enough not to struggle, which would only tighten the noose, and the pull of his hands on the rope was the only thing that prevented him from strangling immediately.

The moment the snare whipped out of the brush catching Matt and pulling him off his feet, both Alex and Cory began racing up the incline to the huge, oak tree that held the other end of the rope, tied at least fifteen feet up the enormous trunk. It was clear that the trunk was much too large to climb and Cory quickly evaluated the situation while he ran. Alex had already reached the tree with his ax when Cory shouted.

"ALEX! CATAPULT ME!"

With uncanny but complete understanding, Alex locked his hands together on his left knee, just as Cory, without breaking stride, slammed his foot onto both hands and, with one incredible movement, Alex thrust him upward into the tree with a groan of unbelievable effort.

The lowest branch of the ancient oak was as thick as a man's waist and only their combined strength lifted him into the air high enough, permitting Cory to wrap his arms around it. From there he swung his legs up and stood where he could just reach the branch above his head to which the rope was tied. Quickly wrapping his left arm around the taut rope above the tie, Cory drew the hunting knife from his belt and, with one smooth stroke, he sliced the knot.

Although he had considered Matt's weight as so much greater than his, he was still surprised when he was jerked off the branch and pulled upward as Matt dropped to the ground. Alex was there to pull the noose from his nearly unconscious brother and Cory, now twenty feet up the tree, tied the rope back on a branch and let himself down.

Alex was pouring water onto his Tshirt and using it to swab Matt's neck and face where he lay on the ground when Cory knelt down beside them. "Is he going to be okay?" he asked.

"I think so," Alex answered in an unconvincing tone. "Thanks to you!" he added.

Cory shook his head as he studied the discolored marks on Matt's neck. " That wasn't me, Alex. That was *US*!" he said.

They were in the process of deciding how to get Matt home when he spoke. "Hey, Pooter…what gives?" he asked in a hoarse and raspy voice. Confusion showed on his face as he attempted to rise on one arm, then fell back down. With a loud groan, he remained flat on his back for a few moments more, then with a slight shake of his head, he sat up and struggled to stand.

"You okay?" Alex asked while he held his arms outward in a gesture that said he thought Matt would fall over any minute.

"Yeah. I think so." he said with a puzzled look. The expression on his face suddenly changed and it was clear that the reality of what had just happened was beginning to be understood. As though exhausted, he slumped onto the skid they had piled with wood, and he ran his hands over his face, touching his neck gingerly where the deep purple bruises were still in the process of forming.

Cory and Alex were so relieved to see him alive and apparently not seriously damaged by the experience, that they began grinning at each other and then broke into happy laughter, ending with a few congratulatory slaps on Matt's back until finally they were rewarded with a slight smile.

Death is a sobering thought and suddenly they all sat in silence, knowing how dreadfully close Matt had come to dying. Without speaking or moving they sat or sprawled on the ground in the warm sun, on a hot August day, letting their eyes take in the blue sky dotted with white clouds that peaked between the trees, each lost in their own thoughts and feeling grateful for life!

Staring at Cory, Matt finally broke the silence.

"I guess...I've been unfair," he began in a voice that sounded as though he had a case of severe laryngitis. "I don't know if...we'll ever be best friends," he continued, struggling to get the words out, "but...I owe you my life! Thanks!" With that, he got up unsteadily and motioned for Alex to start gathering their equipment and firewood. It was time to go home. "By the way..." he added, as he turned around, "nice knife!"

Before they parted, Alex asked Cory not to mention what happened today to any members of his family, including Jenny, explaining that it would only worry their mother and cause a lot of commotion.

Cory agreed. This was the kind of incident that you NEVER told your parents unless you wanted to spend the rest of your life protected and safely confined to your room—permanently!

Winding his way through the forest on his way home, Cory felt the elation that comes with saving someone's life. This must be what firefighters and policemen feel every time they rescue someone, Cory thought. It was a warm, comfortable feeling that stayed with him until he remembered the mother bear and his betrayal of her. Then guilt and sadness overwhelmed his sense of well-being.

One thought led to another and as he reached the cabin, he knew a trip to Annie's was necessary in order to report the bear situation. She needed to know that a wounded bear was no longer a threat. Then, too, Annie often helped Cory see things clearly with her common sense and bits of wisdom. Maybe she could convince him that he had done the right thing about Suzy.

The smell of just-baked bread reached Cory when he was still a good distance from Annie's and the fragrance swept away his despondent feelings. He pictured her beautiful face and felt gratitude in having met her and learning that she was his grandmother.

Hurrying, he arrived in the yard as she was bathing Brute with a push-broom and a hose. Completely covered in suds, Brute stood perfectly still with legs spread while Annie lathered him with the broom and proceeded to rinse him with the spray from the hose. The scene was so comical that Cory couldn't keep from laughing and the moment he began, Brute made a dash for him. Soon both of them were on the ground covered with suds. The always obedient dog ignored all of Annie's commands until she could get to them and pull him off.

"Oh, Cory! I'm so sorry!" she cried, grabbing the dog and pulling him away so Cory could stand up.

"Annie, it's okay!" he responded, laughingly. "He likes me!"

In the end, Cory held Brute, and Annie rinsed both of them, trying not to drench Cory completely.

While Cory and Brute sat in the sun drying off, Annie plied them with treats. Cory's was a huge sandwich on fresh, still-warm bread, filled with slabs of roast beef, slices of tomato and lots of mustard. Brute chewed on his favorite—a new leather bone. Annie handed Cory a huge glass of cold milk and slipped into her comfortable chair on the porch with a cup of strong coffee.

"We need to talk, Cory," she said quietly.

Cory stopped eating and looked up when he heard the seriousness of her tone. "What's wrong, Annie?" he asked hesitantly.

She took a sip of her coffee as they looked at each

other. Cory watched the slight shake of her head before she spoke.

"I can't come to your football game," she finally answered. "I just can't do it."

"Why not?"

There was an unusually long pause.

"I've never been so frightened of anything in my life," she whispered.

Cory set the sandwich on the table and crouched in front of Annie. He took her hands and held them. "You have nothing to fear," he assured her.

"Oh yes I do! There will be hundreds of people there and your father might not be happy to see me. It could be an ugly scene with my son blaming me, all over again, for the death of his family. I can't take the rejection of all those people along with my son. I don't want to move again. I like it here and have finally been able to call it home. Please try to understand," she pleaded.

That was the problem. He DID understand. All he had to do was think of his music and the fear of rejection that went with it. He felt a great sadness for Annie. He really did understand. With a slight squeeze of her hands as he held them, he agreed with her decision not to attend the game and promised her that everything would work out in the end. Her expressive blue eyes showed her gratitude for his understanding and they returned to their refreshments in silence.

Cory sat on the step and leaned against the porch post with Brute overflowing his lap while he soaked in the warmth of home, good food, and the love he always felt at Annie's. "The wounded bear is no longer a threat," he stated bluntly. He swallowed twice before he could begin telling Annie why.

Explaining the capture of the mother bear and his reluctant part in it, revived the painful memory of Suzy's departure from the cabin, locked in a cage. Cory's strong self-discipline was tested several times as he related all that had happened with the mother bear since he had first warned Annie about her.

"The bear trusted me," Cory admitted, sadly. "I'm not sure I did the right thing." He looked at Annie questioningly.

"You don't need me to tell you that you did the right thing," she replied. "You KNOW that you did the right thing. Since you are apparently upset about it, Cory, why don't you check up on her?"

"How? If I call, they can tell me anything they want. It's easy to lie over the phone. They promised me that Suzy would be taken to a veterinarian and then released into the wild when her wound was healed. For all I know, she could already be dead." Cory ended in a frustrated sigh.

"Cory! You are going to spend the night here again," Annie commanded, rising from her chair and grabbing their dirty dishes. She held the screen door open for Brute, who rose to his feet, knowing he wasn't being given a choice. "WE are going to check on Suzy!"

In confusion, Cory watched her grab keys and a small wallet off the kitchen counter, lock the door, and stride purposefully around the side of her cabin while he scurried to keep up with her.

"Our first stop will be the veterinarian in Woodville to see how honest our authorities have been. Then, we head to the grocers to get some food for you since Suzy, I'm sure, has gotten the better part of your food supply."

Annie grinned at Cory as they headed toward the four-wheeler. The grin became contagious as he climbed on behind her and they roared down the lane for four miles to the Jeep. Traveling the six miles on the sandy logging road in the Jeep, brought back memories of

Cory's trip the night he came to the cabin. Happy memories!

When they turned onto the blacktop road to Woodville, Cory sat back with the wind tearing through his overly long blonde hair, and drank in the feel of speed and the open road. He noted, however, that Annie was a cautious driver never exceeding the speed limit and, given the terrible accident in her past, he was surprised that she was willing to drive at all. Although, living as she did would make it necessary.

Cory's faith in, and respect for authorities in general, was greatly advanced as the day progressed. They had kept their word about Suzy, and Cory found her well and active, although still penned at the vet's. Surgery had been performed to remove the bullet and they believed they had located her cub which was, at the moment, being transported. Despite their repeated warnings, Cory let the mother bear lick his hand and then fed her through the fence. It pained him to see her caged, but the pen was large and encircled an area of tall grass similar to her usual surroundings.

Due to Cory's curiosity, they rode passed the Woodville High School and noted the extensive sports fields—football, baseball, track, tennis, and soccer. He wondered if music was even taught at this obviously sports-oriented school.

Although he protested because he had no money with him, Annie insisted on buying enough food to last him the remainder of the summer. As they piled the groceries in the Jeep, Cory couldn't help thinking of the short time he had before the school year began and he returned home. It was a very sobering thought.

They reversed their roles and Cory drove the Jeep back from Woodville after a satisfying meal at a local restaurant. This was the first time he had been in any community, especially one this small, since the beginning of summer and the experience was surprising. He had always considered these little communities to be somewhat backward and yet, Woodville's high school appeared new, large, impressive, and advanced. Cory loved the quiet and separation that living in the woods gave him and the thought of returning home to his old school was not appealing. He thought of all these things as he drove the Jeep and then the four-wheeler back to Annie's cabin.

When they climbed off the machine, they couldn't stop laughing at the grocery bags hanging from their belt loops, around their necks, and over their shoulders and it was already late when the groceries were put away or packaged for Cory's return to his cabin in the morning.

Although he would have been fine with sleeping on the floor as he had done before, he accepted the guest bedroom that Annie offered. However, when she opened the door and invited him in, he stood in awe of the room's interior. Here was the room of a seventeen-year-old boy including all the paraphernalia that went with a sports-minded young man. This was obviously all of his dad's possessions at the time he left home—for good! Cory looked at Annie.

"This is a copy of my dad's room," he said.

Annie nodded, tears clouding the blue of her eyes. Slowly she hugged him and said, "Sleep well, grandson."

Chapter 12

Everything around the cabin resonated with the coming of a new season, and Cory noted each reminder. The ticks had disappeared in July and the raspberries with them. While the water at the lake reached its peak temperature from the direct rays of the sun and the leftover heat of each day, the nights were already getting colder. Migratory birds were flocking together, and antlered deer sported velvet racks that would not grow much larger before shedding their coverings. Crickets chirped while Cory played his guitar each evening and the drying leaves on the trees scratched each other in the wind. Fall was coming.

Cory's father had called earlier this morning to inform him of his arrival later today. He was already in the States arranging the rental of a car and packing for the trip to the cabin. The enthusiasm Cory heard in his dad's voice brought a smile to his face and confirmed that the cabin had become a special place for him, too.

It wasn't until after eight o'clock that evening that the sound of a Jeep could be heard struggling down the lane and into the clearing. Cory was thrilled at the return of his father. During the period of his last visit, they had learned so much about each other and had not engaged in a single argument. For some reason the cabin brought them together peacefully.

Following the usual bear hug and the stowing of gear, Cory and his dad relaxed on the porch in their favorite chairs while stories were exchanged. In the past, Cory had never heard much about his dad's business, but, for some reason, his father seemed to enjoy relating the more interesting events of his travels when he was here at the cabin.

Too much had happened to Cory while his father was away, and he consciously and carefully chose each of his words in order to prevent blurting out anything about Annie since she was so much a part of his life now. They laughed about the skunk and regretted the capture of Suzy, but Cory was silent about checking on the bear and the rescue of Matt. Someday, he would explain both of those events, but now was not the time.

After learning about Annie's fear of meeting her son for the first time in twenty-four years, Cory decided that he would simply force them to meet each other. Unsure of how he would do that, the opportunity suddenly presented itself the next morning shortly after breakfast when the question of loneliness arose. They were washing dishes and cleaning up the cabin when his father voiced his concern.

"You've been here two and a half months," he pointed out. "Except for my short stay, you've been alone. Hasn't that bothered you?"

Cory could hear the worry creep into the question. Was this the time to tell him about Annie? Doubts assailed him. He had promised that he would not tell his father about her, but why shouldn't they be reunited if that was possible? Was it? What if she was right and it only stirred up all the resentment and blame all over again?

His dad was looking at him with concern and waiting for a response while Cory fought with his conscience. If he broke his promise and it turned out badly, Annie would suffer along with his dad, and Cory's relationship with her would be over. The thought of that was unbearable. On the other hand, all three of them had lost so much over a tragedy that occurred too many years ago. With a deep breath, he plunged into the conversation.

"Actually, Dad, I found a friend." Uncertain how to continue, Cory paused.

"You mean Jenny."

"No. I have another friend. She lives just to the north of our property and I'd really like you to meet her. Today!"

The words shot out of Cory's mouth before he knew exactly what he was saying and as he watched his dad, he knew there was no turning back. He hurried to combat the frown that appeared on his father's face.

"She's really nice, Dad, and I know you're really going to like her." Cory was stumbling all over his words. "Let's go this morning. I want you to meet her. She's been good to me and often gives me food." Oh, why didn't he just shut up?

"Cory? Ah…she wouldn't just happen to be about forty years old and very pretty, would she?" his father asked suspiciously.

"Oh…gosh, Dad. No! She's much too old for you." He gave his dad a playful punch on the shoulder and headed toward the door. "Come on! It's a two hour hike, if you think you can make it," he teased.

Like two twins they started down the trail to Annie's, dressed in cargo shorts, hiking boots and T shirts. The only way the father stood out from the son was to see the small lines of worry and tragedy that had begun to mark his face. At the moment, however, they were having fun and even the hike was a contest between them.

Cory pointed out the scenes of some of his adventures as they followed the trail and the encounter with the bear and her cub was relived, but throughout the trek, Cory's thoughts went to Annie and he prayed that this would work out right. NEVER would he intentionally hurt her!

About halfway there, Michael stopped short and Cory, who was walking directly behind him, almost knocked him over.

"Hey! What's the matter?" Cory demanded, catching himself from crushing his dad.

Those startlingly blue eyes stared piercingly into Cory's. "Tell me again, son. This isn't a set-up for your Dear Old Dad to get a girlfriend now, is it?"

Cory simply rolled his eyes skyward and laughed, expressing how absurdly foolish this question was, because he dared not speak. His stomach was in knots and the tension of knowing he could be making a fatal mistake was descending on him in the form of a gigantic headache. Accepting the gestures as an answer, his father swung around and continued down the trail.

When they arrived at Annie's, Cory was in the lead and he spotted her sitting on the porch with Brute at her feet while she worked at something in her hands. Brute was up and chasing toward him the moment they entered the yard and even from a distance, Cory saw the tremble when Annie stood up as she watched them come across the lawn.

She put one hand out to brace herself against the post and stared past Cory. Annie was dressed in her usual jeans, plaid shirt with sleeves rolled to the elbow, and cowboy boots. Her hair was pulled back in a single long braid and whisps of pure white tendrils framed her beautiful face.

Michael had stopped when he saw Annie stand. He seemed frozen to the spot. While Cory held Brute's collar and stepped to the side with him, he watched his father and grandmother see each other for the first time in twenty-four years. Fear swept over him as the tableau in front of him seemed locked in silence.

With shaky steps in slow motion, Annie came down the porch stairs. Her eyes never left her son's face. Giant tears pooled and slid down her cheeks as she stood a few feet away from him.

Michael took a tentative step forward and Cory could see the moisture form in his dad's eyes.

"Can you ever forgive me, mother?" he asked, gently.

"Oh, Michael," she sobbed, "It is I who should be asking YOU for forgiveness."

Two single steps were taken and they wrapped their arms around each other and cried.

Cory took Brute and walked away with tears in his own eyes. He had never seen his father cry and often regarded crying as an act of sissies, but as he watched it now, it didn't seem unmanly. It seemed human!

He took the dog to the other side of the cabin and off into the woods. The tension was gone and replaced with a tremendous feeling of euphoria. He was so happy, he couldn't stop smiling. Wanting to give his father and grandmother enough time to reunite, Cory spent the next hour hiking out to the logging road and back. When he returned to Annie's cabin, he found them huddled in the living room pouring over old photograph albums and laughing about happy memories.

"Oh, Cory, you're the best grandson I could ever hope for," Annie said as she threw her arms around him. He kissed her on the forehead and then received a bear hug from his dad.

"Thanks, son. This is the greatest gift I've ever gotten!"

As they sat around the table for lunch and then returned to the albums, Cory was conscious of the fact that they were a family. They belonged to each other now, and as usual, he could not dismiss the warmth of being at Annie's cabin with its familiar smells of good food and clean towels.

Most of Cory's life was spent in a large, rambling house with no one home, in a city of more than one million people, at a school with two thousand students, and he felt less alone here in the national forest by himself than he did at home. No, that wasn't home. THIS felt like home. Here, with family! While he listened to his dad and grandmother, the thought of returning to the city was almost a physical pain.

Although reluctant to leave, Cory and his father needed to get back to the cabin before dark and they had already pushed their time to the limit. Crossing the lawn, Michael suddenly remembered the football game and turned toward Annie as she stood on the porch.

"Cory will be playing football at the Wharton's tomorrow," he said proudly. "I'll pick you up in the Jeep at nine o'clock in the morning." He continued to look at Annie and then added, "I love you, Mother."

"I love you, too, Michael."

Just before they disappeared into the woods, Annie called out. "Give your father directions, Cory, because I'll have to meet him with the four-wheeler at the logging road."

A wave from each of them signaled their understanding and they hurried into the forest. Like little boys, Cory and his dad trekked through the trees, elated by the day's events. Michael playfully slapped him on the back in happiness each time Cory told another story in his growing relationship with Annie, including how he first met her. Wherever possible, they walked side by side with a father's arm draped across his son's shoulder as Cory explained the many encounters with Annie throughout the summer.

She had explained her confusion when she first saw Cory as he came to her rescue when she was pinned by the fallen tree. To look up and see the face of her son had frightened her until the absent blue eyes suggested a mere coincidence and then she blamed her desire to have her son back for the wild conclusion she had drawn. That's what Annie reasoned at the time, but finding out that Michael was the name of Cory's father stirred her confusion once more. How much can be attributed to coincidence?

Since it was already quite late when they reached the cabin, they broke with their usual routine of sitting on the porch, Michael with his book and Cory with his guitar, and went straight to bed. With the twinge of cold night air slipping through the open window of the loft, Cory pulled another blanket over himself and lay on his back looking at the ceiling. Finally he whispered.

"Are you sleeping, Dad?"

A short, quiet laugh came with the whispered answer.

"Not yet."

"Are you happy, Dad?"

"I'm happy, Cory."

Things had worked out so well that Cory found it difficult to sleep that night. He wanted to replay the events of the day over and over again in his mind. Now that they found Annie and she was a part of their family, why couldn't she come to live with them? Once that thought entered his head, Cory didn't want to let it go. She'd have a home with people who loved her and it would certainly add happiness to their household. He might even look forward to coming home from school each day. The more he visualized the plan, the more awake he felt, and it was well past midnight before he finally fell asleep.

Temperatures plunged during the night and Cory woke long before dawn, closed the loft window and slipped out of bed to throw some kindling into the potbellied stove and start a fire. Crawling back in bed, he huddled under the warmth of the blankets and remembered the football game. It was today!

For the first time in his life, the thought of playing football frightened him instead of boring him. What if he didn't play well? What if he made a fool of himself? Maybe he wouldn't be able to throw accurately. Maybe Pooter, correction, Alex should be quarterback. That's the position Alex plays during the school year for the high school team and Cory is as good a receiver as he is in other positions. Wait! If he doesn't play well, what difference does it make what position he plays?

It was clear that Cory would never get back to sleep. He checked the clock. It was four-thirty! He needed some sleep or he really wouldn't be any good at football. Jenny would be watching him play and he couldn't stand the thought of her seeing him fail. Then too, what about the crowds of people that Jenny said attend this game each year. Although almost all of them would be total strangers to him, they all knew the Whartons and he didn't want to disappoint any of them. It was no help, however, to know that his dad and Annie would be there. That would only be great if he played like a pro. He just had to do well. If he played rotten, he would simply go home after the game. NO! That would be the coward's way. He'd HAVE to stay. Ohhhh… but Jenny's brothers would give him a hard time about his playing.

Surfacing from a deep sleep which he finally slipped into as morning arrived, Cory literally shook himself awake to hear his dad whistling in the kitchen. His father's obvious good mood only served to emphasize Cory's lack of confidence and despondency as he attempted to convince himself that everything would work out fine.

A clear sky was allowing the sun to melt the frost on the lawn sending little spirals of vapor into the air like steam off hot blacktop and Cory stared at it while he stood at the front window. He was worried.

Michael insisted on making him bacon, eggs, and

toast for breakfast even though he had no appetite for it, and when a seventeen-year-old boy refuses a meal, something is obviously disturbing him. True to his nature, his dad chose to wait for Cory to bring up the problem.

"Dad," he said finally when he was seated at the table to eat a breakfast he didn't want. "What if I play badly today?" Before his father had a chance to answer, Cory paraphrased his question, emphasizing the fear he was feeling. "What if I'm really rotten today?"

With the frying pan in his hand in the process of placing eggs on Cory's plate, his father gave him a piercing look when he answered. "You won't be, Cory. I've never seen a young man play as well as you do. Why do you think I've been hounding you to play the game? You are a fantastic athlete and you will be astoundingly good today." With that, he slid three eggs onto Cory's plate and three onto his own and sat down.

While he slowly forced himself to eat, Cory thought of his father's words and tried to accept the faith his father had in him, but he knew from experience that parents usually had no clue as to the true abilities of their children. Cory's musical talent was the best example. As of this moment, his father still has not commented one word about the guitar and Cory's ability to play. It was true that his father's silence on the matter confused Cory and challenged his confidence, but ultimately he knew that he played well and he didn't really need his father's approval. Or did he? In any case, maybe his father wasn't a good judge of his athletic ability either.

As the eggs and toast slid down his throat with absolutely no taste, Cory continued the painful analysis in his mind. Dishes were washed and gear was gathered from habit and little thought. He packed the Jeep with all the items they would need for the day at the Wharton's and eventually accepted the fact that the day would progress whether he wanted it to or not.

In order to halt the destructive thoughts about football that had been plaguing him since last night, Cory tried to concentrate on Annie. His father planned to pick her up after dropping Cory off at the Wharton's, and as they climbed into the Jeep, Cory took the moment to make his suggestion.

"What do you think of asking MY grandmother to live with us, Dad?"

With his hand on the ignition, Michael looked at Cory with a grin, then turned the key. The engine caught and he started down the lane. "You read my mind!" he said. "You read my mind!"

"She really likes it here, Dad. Do you think she'll come with us?"

It was a question they could not answer and the rest of the trip to the Wharton's was filled with guessing. They did not talk about football and Cory was feeling slightly better as they left the sandy logging road and turned onto the blacktop. He had never gone to the Wharton's except through the woods and now, only with the directions that Jenny had written down for them would they be able to find the place.

The trip was taking longer than they had calculated and Michael would have to leave again immediately to reach Annie's by nine. The back seat of the Jeep was piled with folding chairs, football gear, food, jackets for the evening and blankets for the bleachers. As they neared the turnoff, Cory was feeling more relaxed and he felt ready to play football.

Chapter 13

It would have been quite impossible to miss the Wharton's driveway off the main road. Every tree on each side of the lane had, at least, six brightly colored balloons swinging in the wind. Cory grinned. That had to be Jenny. He couldn't picture any of the boys tying anything pretty or colored to a tree.

The scene, as they approached the end of the driveway, astounded Cory. Michael slowed the Jeep to prevent running over anyone. The field to their right was filled with cars, vans, pickups, and one bus. The lawn and yard in front of them swarmed with people, some chasing chickens, others carrying chairs, equipment, coolers, and miscellaneous items. Cory laughed at his dad's expression, but he knew from experience that the disorganization they saw, was not what it seemed. Underneath it all, was orchestrated activity.

When Cory got out of the Jeep, he reached for the items in the car, but his dad interrupted him. "Leave all of that, Cory. I'll unpack it when I return, otherwise I'll be late in getting your grandmother." He spun the Jeep around and headed back to the main road.

The word "grandmother" always sounded so good to Cory, but he didn't use it very often himself. For some reason, she would always be Annie to him—like a nickname of endearment. He just HAD to play well in the football game today, for his dad and for Annie. Watching the jeep disappear down the driveway, Cory turned sharply and nearly knocked Jenny over where she was standing behind him.

Staggering to keep from falling, she started laughing as she grabbed his arm in an attempt to right herself.

"Wow!" she said. "You must have been totally lost in thought, Cory."

"Sorry! I guess I was, but you're going to like the story I have to tell you!"

With those words, he took her arm and directed her to the closest bench where he proceeded to tell her all about his father's reunion with his mother. Cory was right! Jenny's happiness for Annie was reflected in her smile, her eyes, and in the way she held her head as she listened intently to every word he was saying, until Matt interrupted them.

"Hey, you two!" he shouted. "Come on! We have work to do."

Matt had stopped near the porch with a chicken under his arm, then went striding off to a covered enclosure where everyone with a chicken seemed to be headed. As Cory and Jenny got up to join them, she commented nonchalantly.

"For some strange reason, Gobb doesn't seem to be angry with you anymore. In fact, he tore into Truck for making fun of you and your hunting knife the other day. I wonder why. I don't suppose it has anything to do with those horrid bruises around his neck," she said, questioningly.

They had been walking toward the barn where folding chairs were being unloaded, and Cory simply ignored her question. Jenny wisely accepted that some things concerning her brothers were best left as secrets and she pursued it no more.

Emptied of all farm equipment, and scrubbed to a dull cleanliness, the inside of the barn appeared capable of holding the nearly two hundred people that were expected to attend the day's festivities. Cory discovered as they set up the chairs along the perimeter of the walls that this football game brought all the neighbors and families of the entire area together for perhaps the largest celebration of the year.

As they moved from chore to chore in preparation for the day's events, Cory checked his watch in order to catch his father and Annie when they arrived. He wanted them both to meet the Wharton's. While Annie knew about them, Jenny was the only one she had actually met.

When they arrived, it was clear that Doris Wharton and Annie would become good friends and they wandered off deep in conversation. Michael immediately made himself useful by volunteering to help Bill with the field preparations.

No one would be left out when the football game was scheduled to begin at eleven o'clock, following an early light lunch. You were either a player, a spectator, a referee, or a coach. When the big game was over, volleyball and baseball would begin which included many of the adults. However, since little kids, from infants to teens, came with their families, a series of simple games were also planned.

As the grounds of the Wharton complex slowly melted into a scene of organized production, Cory wandered off to help Alex who was setting up tables for lunch. When they finished the last of the chore, they talked about the football game.

"Who's the big, athletic guy standing with Coach Larson?" Cory asked, cautiously.

Alex followed his gaze and frowned. "Well, from what I've heard, that's Coach Larson's secret weapon," He explained in a somewhat sarcastic tone. "I guess he's a new guy who's transferring to our school for his senior year, and from what I've seen, he thinks he's 'big stuff'. He's their new quarterback for the game today."

"But, I thought we had the scrimmage so there would be no surprises," Cory questioned.

"That's what my dad thought too," Alex responded,

while they both watched the new student prove with his actions what Alex had suggested. Every movement the guy made, said he thought everyone was watching him. "Rumor says that he's the new quarterback at school this year."

"But, aren't you…"

"I WAS during my junior year," Alex interrupted, "but it looks like that might have changed."

The light lunch that was offered, depended on who was eating. After watching Alex's older brothers consume at least five sandwiches apiece, along with fruit, cookies, and several cans of soda, Cory, Alex, and Jenny laughed at their own meager sandwiches in awe of the capacity of others.

As lunch was finished, the crowd slowly wandered over to the bleachers and settled in for the big game. There were cushions, umbrellas against the sun, bottles of water, scorecards, and even megaphones to cheer their respective teams. And, to Cory's surprise, the bleachers were evenly filled on both sides of the field by the time they got into their uniforms.

While they stood at the edge of the field with their coach, Mr. Wharton, Cory was grateful that he had, indeed, eaten a light lunch. His stomach was clenched with tension, and he was much too conscious of where Jenny, Annie, and his father sat with Mrs. Wharton on the bleachers. He simply HAD to play well.

The other team won the toss and elected to receive, giving Alex and Cory a chance to observe the new student. Unfortunately, to their dismay, he was good! Exceptionally good! However, two of the Wharton brothers were not only big, but fast, and their efforts at defense proved invaluable, preventing the opposing team from scoring.

When the Wharton offense finally took the field, Cory felt the pressure return. He just HAD to be his best and help his team to win. Since he had never played in organized sports, it never really mattered if he played spectacularly or not. In his physical education classes nobody was that competitive. If they were, the coach would have had them on a team immediately.

Unfortunately, how Cory played today mattered, more than he wanted it to, and he went out on the field with fear rattling his composure. Whether Alex observed his stress or shared in it, Cory never knew, but the constant patter from Alex about how good they were as a team, began to absorb the stress Cory felt.

By the end of the first quarter, Cory had thrown seven beautiful passes and only one interception. It didn't even matter that Alex had read his intentions and been in the right spot at the right time to receive each of the seven passes, because the defense on the other team was as good as the Wharton team, and there still was no score.

After the first successful pass, Cory began to settle down and now only the desire to win fired him with enthusiasm. At first the screams of the fans and the echoing of his name disturbed him, but now he no longer was conscious of the crowd. Since the opposing team seemed to anticipate their plays, Mr. Wharton changed some of them and the second quarter saw the first touchdown from Cory's hands to Alex's.

Conceding that the new student, Jeremy, on the other team, was actually a great football player came with difficulty, and the game progressed painfully with Jeremy throwing three touchdown passes which the Wharton team was unable to stop. They entered the fourth quarter revising some of their plays, once again, while the score stood at twenty-one to seven.

Cory had never inquired, but he had always assumed

that Mr. Wharton was a real coach of some sport or at least an assistant coach. Now, he was convinced. No one could know as much about football as he did and not be involved with it on a regular basis. He also anticipated some of the plays of the opposing team and because of that, the fourth quarter began with two touchdowns by the Wharton team. The score was now tied and the fans on both sides of the field were in a frenzy.

Winning was now everything, and for the first time, Cory was enjoying the desire to win a football game. It was closing in on the last quarter with THIRTY SECONDS left in the game. Play was on the fifty-yard-line, and the Wharton team was in possession. With a motion from his coach, Cory called for their last time-out and the team went to the sideline. After a few brief words from Mr. Wharton, the team began moving onto the field, but he held Cory back a moment.

Grabbing both of Cory's arms and looking him straight in the face, he said, "I'm sending Alex into the end zone for this next play. You gotta rifle that ball right down the field, son. It's our only chance to win and they'll never expect it."

"Coach! There's no way I can throw that far," Cory protested. "You're asking me to do the impossible."

But Mr. Wharton was already turning away and Cory had no choice but to try his best.

Back on the field, he got ready for the snap and thought of the day he had pelted Alex with mud balls from the swamp. They had come a long way to become friends and now he was being asked to perform the impossible with Alex's help. Suddenly Cory pictured the swamp and his body covered with mud. He had been so angry with Pooter that day. Think of it now, he said to himself. It's Pooter laughing at you at the end of the field. He deserves to be pelted with mud.

As the ball hit his hands, his reflexes took over and while Matt and the rest of the team protected him, he drew back with his arm and, summoning all the strength he could gather, whipped the ball into the air in a direct line toward Pooter. With dread, yet unsupported hope, he watched it spiral in slow motion upward and over the other players, then down and eventually right into Alex's hands standing open in the end zone. The crowds on both sides of the field went wild.

The game was over!

In a period of one day, all sports were suddenly seen by Cory from a different perspective. It wasn't the fact that the football team carried him and Alex off the field on their shoulders in celebration, or his teaming with his father against the two coaches in soccer, or his coaching of the ten to twelve-year-old volleyball team. It was the extraordinary sense of fun mixed with competitive zeal that pointed his opinion of organized sports in another direction.

When he and Jenny helped the three to five-year-olds scrounge for coins in a pile of sawdust, they not only wound up laughing until tears formed, but Cory discovered the true value of sports. He saw five-year-olds share their hoard of money with the younger ones and even step aside when they found a quarter, only to guide a three-year-old to the same discovery. As they brushed the little ones off, righted those who fell, and snuck fresh coins into the pile without being observed, Cory could not help beaming. These were the sports worth playing.

Dinner at the Wharton's for approximately two hundred people seemed a formidable task, but huge table-like grills were set up to cook chicken, hamburgers, and hotdogs with enough hot coals left over for the inevitable marshmallows at the end of the meal. Every family had brought a dish to pass and the end result was a fantastic feast spread out over ten tables set up in one long procession.

After helping the cooks, Tom, Nick, and Greg, Cory wandered to the edge of the crowd and sat on a bench with a huge plate of food. His appetite was back and he needed to remove himself from the barrage of compliments on his football ability. During the game, he had been so wrapped up in the plays that he had not been aware of the praise and applause from the bleachers, but it came with regularity as he moved around the grounds since the game. He wondered if people realized how important ALL the players were. Having been sacked only once in the game, and then receiving an apology from Matt for not preventing it, was a tribute to the players who protected their quarterback. No one played the game alone.

Cory was startled out of his thoughts when Jenny slid onto the bench next to him.

"Hi!" she said. "Isn't this a great day?"

He smiled and nodded. "I was just thinking the same thing."

"It's been a great summer, too, hasn't it?"

Cory paused. "Actually, it's over, Jenny. My school starts in a week, right after Labor Day, and we're leaving the cabin on Wednesday"

"This Wednesday?" She turned to look at him, surprise and unhappiness written on her face.

He nodded and became silent. He felt her hand slide into his.

"I'm sorry for having been such a jerk at the beginning of summer," she confessed. "You're a pretty special guy, Cory Redlam, and I'm not talking about how well you play football. I'm going to miss you when you leave."

Having said that, Jenny got up from the bench and went into the house. A short time later, he saw her appear on the porch with a change of clothing. Jeans and a hooded shirt replaced the shorts and tee, and hair that was pinned back for the day was loose and bounced on her shoulders when she walked to the barn. Others in the crowd got similar clothing from their cars to combat the chill of early evening, for the celebration was not over yet.

Cory and his dad watched from the edge of the confusion, along with most of the men, while the women, in a flurry of activity, packed coolers, put away food, removed dishes and cleaned up the mess of dinner. Michael drew Cory's attention to Annie who was obviously having a wonderful time helping Doris carry a huge tray of leftover chicken into the house.

"I asked your grandmother to come and live with us, Cory," his father said without looking at him.

"I can tell by your voice, Dad, that the answer was, no."

"Don't blame her, Cory," he answered, turning to look at him. "She has had a great deal of pain in her life, and you were right. She loves it here in the woods. It has been her haven for the last twenty-one years. I'm insisting that she get a phone and I intend to ask the Whartons if they wouldn't mind occasionally checking on her. Bill and Doris are special people and I think they already like Annie so I'm sure they will be happy to help."

"Would it be possible for us to come to the cabin for Christmas, Dad? We could invite Annie and make it a real family gathering."

His dad smiled. "I think that could be arranged," he said.

At dusk the crowd slowly moved into the barn for an evening of dancing. Although the highlight of the day was certainly the football game, only a short ceremony at the very end of the dancing was set aside to recognize the winning team. In the far corner of the wooden floor a platform had been built on which a number of chairs and music stands had been arranged. A set of drums was in place and a few instruments on stands or in cases were spread among the chairs.

Cory had never danced much and wondered what type of dancing these people enjoyed. It was impossible to tell from the instruments he saw, but he hoped it wasn't going to be the old-fashioned square dancing that people in small communities seemed to like. He was deciding that he would do the watching while others did the dancing when a voice behind him enquired.

"Do you dance often, Monsieur?" Jenny giggled.

"Not if I can help it," was Cory's joking response, when a sudden sobering thought struck him. Standing next to her, he realized how nice her tallness would fit into his arms if they were ever to dance together. He dismissed the thought as foolish.

"Don't you like music?" she asked, seriously.

Just at that moment, Cory was saved from answering the loaded question by the insistent rapping of Mr. Wharton as he stood on the platform banging on a music stand.

"ATTENTION! Attention, everybody!" He waited for the large crowd of people to find a place to sit or move so everyone could see. Then he calmly waited again for the buzz of talk to quiet and silence to be achieved.

"Would Cory Redlam please come up here?" he announced.

In confusion, Cory turned to look at Jenny. She shrugged her shoulders and shook her head. She obviously had no more idea than Cory as to what was going on.

Mr. Wharton repeated his request and Cory slowly

made his way to the front. Puzzled by all of this, Cory stopped a few feet from the platform at the same time that he saw his father step from the crowd. While he stared at the guitar in his father's hands, Cory was barely conscious of Mr. Wharton's next words.

"My friends," he said, "we have a really special treat this evening. Our star football player, Cory Redlam, will play a number of musical pieces on the guitar."

Is it possible for a person's life to disintegrate in one devastating moment? Cory felt his heart pounding in his chest as he stared first at his father and then at the guitar. How could his dad do this to him? Everything that he had protected all summer was now going to be destroyed in one awful evening and there was nothing he could do about it. While his hands shook and his heart pounded, he finally took the guitar from his father's outstretched arms and stared angrily at the blue eyes. He was so miserable, he could not speak. He stood there for so long that it took several minutes for the chanting voices to penetrate his mind. Everyone, including the Wharton brothers, were shouting for him to play. They couldn't wait for him to make of fool of himself Cory thought, and although it took a whole summer, they would have the ultimate laugh at him now in front of everyone, including Jenny.

Someone had placed a chair at the very front of the platform and in abject misery, Cory moved to sit on it. More than anything he wanted to leave, but only a coward would run from the trouble he was in now. He shifted his long legs, ran a hand through his unruly blond hair, and pulled the guitar into position. The room was suddenly silent in anticipation.

Without any written music, Cory would have to play only the pieces that he knew from memory and in a perverse sense of accommodation, he decided to shock his audience with the classical music first instead of his usual popular to classic method. If they wanted a good laugh, let them start with the music most people disliked.

The moment his fingers touched the strings, however, the tensions of Cory's world fell away and his nimble fingers plucked the strings to his favorite Latin rhythm of "Bolero." As the music flowed through the barn, permeating every crack and space, filling everyone's mind and seeping into the outside air, Cory began to gently smile. He closed his eyes and felt the music soothe his very soul.

In reverse he played the classical, moved to the easy-listening-instrumental pieces, and eventually turned to the well-remembered musicals of the last century. When he finished, he opened his eyes to thunderous applause. At the side of his vision, however, he saw the Wharton brothers slapping each other on their backs and rocking in laughter along with Jenny. Although she was pointing to Matt, the sight of her laughing drove a physical pain into his chest. They would call him whimp again and the whole summer would be lost. Despite the cheering of the rest of the people, Cory heard nothing but the laughter of Jenny and her brothers. He rose slowly from the chair and wound his way through the crowd and out the barn door without seeing a single face. He didn't want to meet his dad or Annie or talk to them. He didn't want to talk at all. The only thing he wanted was to return to the cabin and be alone. But that was not to be.

"Wait, Cory!" Jenny shouted as she broke through the crowd at the barn door and came running after him across the lawn. "Wait!"

"You don't understand," she cried breathlessly as she reached him.

Ignoring her, Cory kept his stride toward the path through the woods. He intended to walk home in the dark with the trees hiding him from the ridicule he felt.

"Wait, Cory!" she persisted. "Let me explain something."

He turned on her then, with anger in his voice. "Why? So you and your brothers can have a good laugh? I get the picture. In your family, everyone who plays a musical instrument is a whimp!"

She started laughing harder and Cory just stood there in stunned silence as he looked at her. In anger and disgust, he turned to leave, but she threw her arms around his neck and buried her face into his shoulder to stop him. Cory couldn't tell if she was still laughing or crying.

Finally she pulled her head back without letting go and stared at him. "The joke is on *US*, Cory! Not you! My brothers spent the entire summer hiding a secret from you. ALL the Whartons are MUSICIANS, Cory! Every one of us!" Watching his face, she released him and stepped back.

"I guess that means ALL the Whartons are whimps!" she giggled, then broke into laughter. When she saw the look of total confusion on Cory's face she laughed even harder. "Don't… you understand?" she managed to ask with a sigh as she brushed a tear of laughter from her face with the back of her hand. "My brothers WANT their tough image and NEVER tell strangers that they love music. They're afraid it will make them seem weak. They even make me promise never to say a word. Everyone who KNOWS *US* is aware of our love of music, but no one talks about it. They understand how the boys feel. My dad is head of the music department at school. He teaches a marching band, a symphony orchestra, and a little jazz group."

Cory's mind reeled with Jenny's words. At first, she wasn't making sense. Then slowly things fit together and he realized that the joke was also on him for trying so desperately to keep his love of music a secret from them.

"We weren't laughing at you, Cory. We were laughing at ourselves."

The look on Jenny's face pleaded with him to understand.

"You play the guitar beautifully," she said, drawing the last word out for emphasis. "Your performance was perfect, and I think my dad is still standing in the barn with his mouth open in admiration and surprise."

The visual picture of Mr. Wharton with his mouth hanging open was too much for them, and they both broke into laughter, dissolving the anger and tension of the evening.

For a long time they sat on the porch swing, talking about music. Cory revealed his dream of being a classical guitarist and for once, he was not pressured to explain or defend his choice. Although Jenny was brought up in a musical family, her goal in life was to become a teacher or social worker, and at sixteen, she had not finalized her choice. They discussed their respective schools and compared the differences. It was obvious that Jenny had formed more friendships in her small school with only five hundred students, than Cory did out of a much larger enrollment. Without any discomfort, they even talked easily about football, in general, and today's game in particular, until the music from the barn brought them back to the present.

"That's pretty good music. Who's playing?" Cory asked with respect clearly indicated in his tone.

"Well, Dad has to be conducting, Mom is at the key board, Matt at trumpet, Alex at the drums, Nick is playing the bass, Tom on the French horn, and Greg plays the violin. The rest of the orchestra is everyone from freshman in high school to Mr. Broder, our eighty-one-year-old neighbor." Jenny smiled. "Last year, Dad started a community band with any adult who was interested."

She sighed. "Dad sure loves his music."

"And, what do YOU play?"

"Flute! But come on! Let's return to the barn. Dad will kill me for not doing my part," she said as she pulled him from the swing and they hurried back to the music.

It was a full day and a long night by the time Cory and his father brought Annie to her house and returned to their own cabin, allowing them to slip into bed by two o'clock in the morning, exhausted by the events of the last twenty-four hours.

And Cory was right! Jenny's height had fit just perfectly into his arms as they danced.

Chapter 14

Cool, clear nights and warm, dry days were normal for the last part of August in the northern forests. Although they had received quite a lot of rain only a week ago, the shrubs and grasses of the clearing around the cabin displayed the parched beige color of fall and snapped with the brittle sound of autumn as they crunched underfoot. They seemed to know that summertime was almost over, and with the first killing frost, most of the small growth would shrivel and die.

Although it was early in the morning, Cory sat in the rocker on the porch slowly strumming his guitar and thinking of yesterday. His father had taken off in the Jeep more than an hour ago to pick up Annie. Michael was determined to get his mother a cell phone and they were driving to Woodville for that purpose. Before he and Cory returned to the city and home, he wanted to be certain that Annie was safe and comfortable until Christmas when they would be together again.

Learning that Annie refused to live with them, had upset Cory at first, but on further reflection, he realized that she was absolutely right. As much as she loved them, it would be HER life that made all the concessions in the move, and with their schedules, she would often still be alone…in a strange house. But Christmas was four months away and in that length of time, Cory would certainly miss Annie.

Yesterday had been an extraordinary day that tested ALL of Cory's emotions, ending on a wonderful, positive high, and it would never be forgotten. Bringing Annie home at midnight, Cory finally had an opportunity to confront his dad about the guitar and was surprised at his response.

When asked why he had never commented on Cory's playing or even argued about it as they had done in the past, his father had said, "I'm not a musician, Cory. No matter how incredible I thought you played, my praise would have meant very little, so I said nothing. You needed to hear it from those who are qualified, and when I learned that the Whartons were experts, I chose to let them hear you. I didn't realize that you might be angry about it or I would never have exposed your talent."

"That's all right, Dad," Cory had replied. "Sometimes we make those kinds of decisions because we love someone," he said, remembering Annie, "and then we pray it will work out right. And it did!"

The most shocking surprise of yesterday had been Jenny's brothers. To see them in an orchestra, displaying remarkable talent with different instruments, had astonished Cory. Not only were they proficient with their first instrument of choice, but each of them could switch to others and play as well.

During intermission, Matt and Alex had joined Cory in the yard along with Greg, Nick, and Tom where they could cool down from the heat generated by the crowd dancing under the lights in the barn. It was at that time that Cory knew he had succeeded in making friends with the Wharton brothers. They exchanged compliments on each other's musical talents, and discussed their plans for the future. When the three oldest boys left them, Matt looked furtively around before thanking Cory for keeping silent about their little "experience" in the woods, and admitted his gratitude for Cory's part in saving his life.

Now, as Cory reminisced about the big football game and a celebration he would remember for the rest of his life, he thought about Jenny and how much she meant to him. He smiled at the thought of their first few meetings, and marveled at the change in his perception as he got to know her better. They had made each other angry so many times, but when forced to leave the cabin on Wednesday, he would remember this incredible girl as kind, intelligent, brave, loving, and forgiving. She was loyal to her family and although her brothers were capable of torturing her with their teasing, she loved them and would rise to defend them at any moment.

The reminder that they were getting ready to leave in just a few days brought him back to the present and Cory despondently hung the guitar in its usual place to start the chores he had planned for today. He cut the grass for the last time, and as he removed each of his troughs from the lawn, he put them across the rafters of the shed to be used again next summer. His makeshift shower would stay for four more days before being dismantled and packed away. Each small action in the process of closing up the cabin for the winter, slid him further into an unhappy mood.

Since Cory was already missing the first weeks of football practice at his school, he provided no argument to his father's suggestion that they spend most of their remaining days at the cabin in honing his athletic skills. Therefore, the afternoon was spent in running, passing, and calisthenics.

When Cory was quite young his father had begun teaching his son the basic skills of each sport and as his natural proficiency surfaced, the sessions became regimented exercises in self-discipline and the techniques. However, it was never a matter of his father acting as a coach with commands being made from the sideline. Instead, it was two athletes, side by side, practicing and improving their game.

Things had not changed much over the years in regard to Cory's training and, in the hot afternoon sun, sweat poured off their bodies as they ran and threw the football, each challenging the other with longer and more forceful passes. As they continued their workout, Cory was more fully conscious of his father's tremendous skill and for the first time he realized how damaging it had been when he tore up his left knee in a college football game, permanently ruining his chances to play in the pros. That sudden realization explained his father's obsession with the idea that his son should be a football player, and increased Cory's desire to please him.

Catching a short but powerful pass, Michael groaned with the effort and then tossed the ball to the side and slumped to the lawn. "I'm getting too old, Cory," he said, grinning as he lay flat on his back looking at the sky. "Your old dad just doesn't have what it takes anymore," he added in a more sobering tone.

Uncertain whether his father was joking or not, Cory joined him on the lawn for a much needed break in their practice.

"You know what they say about cheese, Dad."

"No. What?"

"It gets better with age!"

"I don't think my body agrees with that."

The sound of an engine, along with some scraping and banging noises interrupted their conversation and they sat up in time to see an old, large sedan bouncing over the ruts and clumps of bushes as it came through the trees and into the clearing. The driver was struggling to keep the vehicle within the narrow worn tracks of the lane while he drove fast enough to force his way through the obstacles.

Cory and his father got up and walked toward their unusual visitor, as he got out of the car wearing a full dress suit with a leather briefcase under his arm.

"Hello!" he said. "I hope I have the right place. Mr. Wharton gave me directions, but I'm afraid I missed your driveway several times. I don't think he knew about the little iron gate that is cleverly hidden in the brush," he added with a weak laugh.

"I'm Laurence Millinberg," he explained, reaching out to shake hands with them. "And, this must be Cory?"

"Yes, sir," Cory answered with a frown, puzzled by this stranger with the business-like appearance.

Mr. Millinberg seemed to be in a hurry and with a brief nod, he plunged ahead to explain his purpose in coming.

"I spent the entire day at the Wharton's yesterday," he began, "and I must say, that was some celebration! But to get to the point. I was totally impressed with your playing, young man. Anyone with your superior skills should be thinking of a college that would help you enhance your abilities." He paused to take a breath and then went on.

"You see, I am a scout for Benningham College," he announced proudly, "and I am prepared to offer you a four-year, comprehensive scholarship to our fine institution. That means EVERYTHING would be paid for, son, including tuition, room and board, books, and even equipment," he beamed. "We are one of the finest private colleges in the east and you couldn't do better."

Cory was staring at his father during the last of Mr. Millinberg's speech, knowing that this had something to do with him. No scout would have been accidentally at the Wharton's football game. His father must have arranged it. Had he and his dad misunderstood each other once again? When Cory agreed to play football his senior year, he didn't realize it would require a four-year college commitment too. How foolish he was! Of course, he'd have to play another four years! What was he thinking? He felt anger rising at himself for being so naïve and at his dad for pushing him to make a choice he didn't want. He needed some time to absorb all of this and rethink his commitment.

"I'm not sure I want to play football," he said defiantly to an expectant Mr. Millinberg.

Cory saw the expression change from a look of self-satisfaction to confusion.

"I…think…you might be confused," Mr. Millinberg said, with a frown. "I'm NOT offering you a football scholarship!" He paused a moment to let that sink in.

Cory's mind went blank. What was this man talking about? First, he offers a scholarship and then he takes it back? What's going on? He looked at his dad for an explanation, but his father was intently watching Mr. Millinberg who took a deep breath and plowed ahead as though he was striking a difficult business deal.

"I'm here to offer you a MUSIC scholarship, and I might add that we don't do this for just anyone." His tone was defensive now. "Benningham College is devoted to the encouragement and enhancement of the arts. Our music department is rated among the very best in the country. We…"

His voice trailed off with the sentence unfinished while he stared in confusion at the grin on Cory's face. Without another word, Michael took each of them by the arm and propelled them back to the cabin where a music scholarship was discussed and dissected at length.

When Mr. Millinberg's sedan groaned its way toward the logging road with a briefcase containing signed papers, Cory stood with his father on the lawn in front of the cabin staring at the black exhaust belching from the tailpipe of the car as its driver gunned the engine in order to force the bulk of its frame through the shrubs and saplings.

"We need to talk, Dad," he pointed out emphatically.

"I suppose we do," his father responded as though he was talking to himself.

Slipping into their suits, they headed to the lake, walking slowly, unlike their usual race.

A soft breeze swept across the surface of the water, cooling the warmth of the late August winds, as they sat on the dock.

"A boy becomes a man when he learns to care about others, to be brave, to be honest, to love, to work hard, and to forgive," Cory recited. He turned to his father. "Man to man, Dad. Tell me why you and I just signed the papers that would give me a four-year scholarship to a music school when you, obviously, want me to play football?"

His father looked at Cory and studied his face with his piercing blue eyes. "You might find it hard to believe, Cory, given my past behavior, but I truly want you to be happy in whatever you choose in life. You have always been a terrific athlete and happiness comes when we do what suits our abilities so I naturally pushed you to do that."

"What made you change your mind?"

"The night you played the guitar here on the dock, and I saw the smile on your face and heard the astounding music that came from your hands. I knew then that a football was not what you should be holding."

"Why didn't you tell me?"

"I wanted to, but for selfish reasons I needed to have time to readjust my thinking. My goals for you had been so firmly intrenched in my mind that I just couldn't give up the dream in an instant."

There was a long pause as each thought about the other's words.

"It's tough being a parent sometimes, Cory. We make choices that we think are right at the time, and only later discover that it was a mistake. I'm thinking the choice I made when I called up Mr. Millinberg was a good one.

Was I right?"

Cory was too choked up to speak so he simply met his father's gaze and nodded in gratitude.

While they read by candlelight so much earlier than usual that evening, a solid overcast sky promised a much-needed rain that never came. It was hard to believe that in two more months it would be dark at four-thirty in the afternoon. Before going to bed, they discussed and disagreed about bringing electricity into the cabin for next summer and their brief stay at Christmas. Cory's summer had been so special to him that he wanted everything at the cabin to stay exactly the same, while his father thought improvements would make the experience at the cabin so much better. In a compromise, they tabled the decision until both of them had time to study the idea.

With caulking supplies from the hardware store in Woodville, Cory and his father spent all of Saturday filling the cracks in the logs and plugging any hole the size of a pencil eraser that experts boasted were large enough for mice to enter. Determined to keep the critters out, they went at the task with unstoppable energy. Then, because nothing had been done in ten years to protect the log siding, they brushed a finish on the entire cabin, completing the job in time for a farewell dinner with Annie on Monday.

With their standard gift of three small fish, Cory and his dad started out about midmorning for Annie's cabin under the persistently overcast sky. It was depressing for both of them to hike the familiar trail, knowing it would be the last time they did it until the following summer. While hiking, Cory was reminded of the mother bear and her cub as they passed the various places that he had encountered them—once with Jenny. What an extraordinary summer!

Annie had outdone herself. They were still a distance away when the smells of fresh baked bread, and other delicious foods engulfed them on the trail. Clearing the woods, they were eagerly met by Brute who seemed to know that this was a very special occasion. Despite the sadness of a farewell dinner, Annie had decorated the cabin with balloons and streamers tacked on trees, the siding, the porch, the door, and even the interior of the cabin.

Quick hugs and a little teasing about the obvious grand feast they were going to be served, improved Cory's mood and soon he was grinning with pleasure over the wonderful feelings of love and companionship he always felt at Annie's. To his delight, the huge dinner, which they ate at noon to accommodate the long trek home before dark, ended with a dessert that appeared too beautiful to cut.

"What do you call this creation, mother?" Michael asked when she proudly carried it to the table.

It stood at least a foot high and had swirls of hard chocolate cleverly designed over a base of creamy white something-or-other. Looking more like a piece of art than anything edible, Cory slipped a finger into the side and discovered that his father had already done so as they both licked the scrumptious dessert.

"Now, you two stop that until I cut it!" Annie said in a fake scold. "This," she announced proudly, "is my WELCOME HOME dessert."

Slightly confused, Cory laughed. "I hate to inform you, grandmother, but, if you had planned to send this dessert to our house in the city to welcome us home, it wouldn't have made it."

He started to laugh again when he caught the look on his father's face, clearly indicating that his dad knew something Cory didn't. He folded his arms and sat back in the chair.

"Okay, what's the punch line?" he asked, "I seem to be the only one not getting the joke."

"No joke, Cory," Annie said as she set the huge dessert directly in front of him. "This is a welcome home dessert if YOU want it to be. Your father and I have discussed the subject and we are both in agreement that you should live with ME this winter and attend Woodville High School. I know the school is smaller than you're used to and the cabin is not as..."

She never completed her sentence because Cory had jumped up to sweep her off her feet in a bear hug that almost smothered her. Carefully he set her down and pulled out a chair so she would not fall over from her laughter. HE was too happy to speak.

For the remainder of the afternoon, Cory lay propped on a pile of pillows next to Brute on the floor and listened to his grandmother and his dad talk about old things, new things, and everything in between. They agreed that Cory would go home on Wednesday to pack his things and bring them back the following day. Since his father would not hear of his mother being at the cabin without a vehicle, he intended to purchase a four-wheel-drive SUV for Cory to return to Annie's. That way he would have transportation to school and a second car provided extra safety in the event that Annie's Jeep did not start. Of course, a second snowmobile and a second four-wheeler would also have to be purchased so that either of them could be off somewhere without the other one stranded.

One thought led to another and the afternoon sped by in a flurry of planning. Annie was thrilled when informed of the scholarship that Cory had been offered to pursue his love of music at a special college dedicated to that purpose, but she was subdued at the reminder that Cory would spend only one school year with her. However, it was clear from the look in her eyes that she was grateful and happy to be with her family again.

When Michael and Annie became entrenched in a deep conversation about the past, Cory allowed himself to slip into a light doze. His stomach was satisfied, the pillows were soft, and the steady rhthym of the dog sleeping next to him on the floor, spelled HOME. What more could he possibly want? With a smile on his face, he lay half asleep only slightly aware of the other two people in the cabin.

However, he pulled himself back to full consciousness when he heard his father mention the differences in their names.

"I deeply regret the name change, mother," Michael was saying, "and I've looked into changing it back, but it actually shouldn't be done at this time. I have my name on so many business documents that are involved with other large corporations in the process of mergers. It would not only complicate matters, but might even ruin the deals, and others would be hurt by the change.

"Michael, I don't need you to change your name," his mother replied. "I really do understand how you felt when your father and sister were killed in the accident, and our reunion is all I care about. I couldn't be happier. I have a son and grandson in my life now, and nothing could bring me greater joy."

Cory never heard the rest. He was sound asleep.

Chapter 15

Sometime after midnight, a soft, light rain began to fall, bringing its sweet smell through the open window near Cory's head. He gently rolled over on his pile of blankets covering the pinecone mattress, and thought about the changes that this short summer had brought to his life. So much had happened. He came to the cabin to make a choice, never realizing that one choice would lead to others. But the contentment he felt now, proved that the decisions that had been made were correct.

Today they would complete their packing, store the shower, and remove all the furniture from the porch. The interior of the cabin would receive attention during the major portion of the afternoon, making sure that things were clean and all food removed to discourage the critters who would be seeking refuge for the long winter. Along with the invitation to stay with Annie for the school year came the agreement that Christmas would be spent at her place, so they would not be using the cabin again until the following summer.

Stopping at the Wharton's for goodbyes as they left tomorrow morning, was actually his father's suggestion, and although he pretended to be nonchalant about it, Cory was eager to do so. He wanted Jenny to know that it was a temporary goodbye, and he would be back in time for the first day of school. Anticipating his desire to stay, his father had already enrolled him at Woodville, and records were in the process of being transferred to his new school.

Because of the special football game at the Wharton's last Thursday, Cory already knew about half of his future senior classmates—more than he ever knew in any of his former classes, and Woodville High School didn't feel like a new, strange school. Having Alex in his class and with Jenny being a junior, Cory would never feel alone at Woodville High.

The brief overnight rain pulled some of the dead leaves from the trees and teased the grass with the possibility of renewed growth, but it left something undesirable as well. Coming back from an early morning trek to the creek for water, Michael reported the discovery of fresh tracks in the damp earth near Cory's pier. The cougar was back!

"We need to remind the Whartons of the danger when we see them tomorrow," his father stated with concern in his voice and a frown on his face. "I wish people would take the warnings seriously," he added.

"Mr. and Mrs. Wharton took it seriously when I showed them my digital pictures," Cory declared. "They won't allow Jenny to hike in the woods without one of her brothers."

"I wonder how much safer that is," Michael replied. "If the boys don't carry a weapon, how can they protect themselves, or her? And didn't you tell me that her brothers considered it one big joke?"

The discussion about the cougar continued through breakfast and surfaced again several times as the packing and storing of items kept them physically busy. Cory had no answer to his father's worry. The cat had been a problem all summer and yet, no one ever saw it, except Cory, and then only for a brief moment, and not clearly.

"Mountain lions, or cougars are usually shy creatures and hunt mainly at night," his father pointed out as they took the shower apart and put the pieces in storage. "But they have the bad habit of reacting when anything moves quickly. Once something runs, the cougar's instincts kick in and it gives chase because it sees the moving object suddenly as prey."

Stopping in the middle of his work, Cory stared at his dad. "If you're trying to impress me with the danger, or frighten me for Jenny's sake, you're doing an excellent job," he said sarcastically.

"Sorry. I just don't want to forget to have a talk with the Whartons tomorrow. We'll both have to convince them that the danger is real."

Before storing the lawn mower for next summer, Cory sharpened the blades and cleaned it. Once everything was put away, Michael boarded up the shed-like garage and sitting on the steps of the porch they cleaned the guns and placed them back into their leather cases to hang in the summer kitchen out of sight. Ammunition was stored above the kitchen cabinets and all the tools that Cory had used over the summer were cleaned and packed between newspapers to keep them dry in the bottom of a wooden trunk.

Since the pine cones of Cory's bed were a food source for a number of small critters, Michael carried the homemade mattress into the woods and shook the smashed and crumbled pieces from the burlap bags. For one night, Cory would sleep on the floor of the loft and later, new beds would be purchased for their return next summer.

It was late afternoon when they completed the cleaning of the kitchen and packed all the remaining food into the cooler. As they checked things off their list and concentrated on not missing any task, they heard the drone and surge of engine power, announcing the arrival of a visitor.

Standing on the porch, Cory watched Matt pull a pickup into the yard, cut the engine, and step out of the vehicle.

"Hey!" he shouted, "Jenny hasn't been here, has she?"

Cory heard the concern in his voice, noted the clenched fists, and saw the worried look on his face, despite Matt's attempt to ask in a casual manner.

"No! We haven't seen her since the party on Thursday," Cory responded as he stepped from the porch and walked toward Matt. "Why? Was she coming here today?"

"Well…I'm…not sure," Matt stammered.

"What's going on, Matt?" Cory demanded. "I can see that something's wrong."

While Matt shifted his stance from one leg to the other and ran a hand over his face, pushing the hair back from his forehead, a sense of dread was seeping into Cory's consciousness. He repeated the question.

"What's wrong? Where's Jenny?"

Matt stared miserably at Cory. Michael joined them in time to hear his answer.

"We don't know! She was supposed to bring us lunch this noon but she never showed up."

"Where?"

"Northeast of our place where we're cutting the last of the firewood."

Matt's answers were laced with worry and he stood there, six-foot-four and all two-hundred-sixty-seven pounds of him, looking like a sad little boy who had just lost his puppy.

"When was she supposed to be there?" Cory asked with fear replacing his worry.

"Noon! She was supposed to be there by noon."

"But, Matt!" Cory cried emphatically. "That's FOUR HOURS ago!"

"I know! We're trying to figure out where she might have gone. Greg is driving to Annie's to see if Jenny might be there, and we're calling all her friends and some of the nei…"

Cory interrupted him as he sucked in his breath and exhaled two words.

"THE COUGAR!"

With his words tumbling over themselves in his hurry to get them out, Cory asked, "Matt, were you and your brothers placing cougar tracks all over the woods to scare Jenny?"

"Look!" Matt said, defensively. "We might tease Jenny but we'd never do anything to hurt her. None of us has even seen any cougar tracks. Besides, there aren't any cougars in this part of the country," he argued sharply.

Grabbing Matt by the front of his shirt, Cory turned and started pulling him as he spoke angrily. "Come on, Matt! I'll show you cougar tracks! Come on! Hurry!"

As Cory let go of Matt's shirt and tore to the creek, he heard the other two right behind him.

Michael pulled some of the tall grasses aside to let Matt view the large, deep impressions of cat paws in the wet sand along the creek that he had discovered that morning. Cory's insides churned as he stared at the number of prints he saw when his father continued to pull aside the grass and point out more. He could not voice the question that his mind repeated. Could there be more than one cat? The possibility drove fear through his chest and almost choked him. He swallowed to dislodge the lump in his throat and looked at his father. The blue eyes confirmed that the same possibility had crossed his dad's mind.

Crouching to place his closed fist into the huge print, Matt muttered, "We've got to find her!"

Directions and decisions were thrown back and forth as they hurriedly returned to the cabin and their vehicles.

"Maybe she's already back home," Matt suggested hopefully as he got into the pickup and started the engine. "Somebody might have found her by now."

"We'll follow you to your place," Michael shouted, backing the Jeep from its spot on the lawn.

Why does everything take twice as long when you're in a hurry? Were they never going to get to the Wharton's? With Michael driving the Jeep, Cory had time to think—too much time. The cougar tracks were real. That much was clear. Matt was not that good an actor to carry the joke this far, and it was evident how frightening the size of the prints had been to him.

Despite Jenny's ability to be feisty, and her courage to stand up for what she believed was right, she generally obeyed her parents. Matt implied that she was asked to bring them their lunch. Why didn't she? Maybe she just had a slight accident—a fallen tree pinning her down like it did to Annie? Or, the cougar! Would she run from the animal? Most people did and the results were deadly.

Repeated efforts to dismiss the thought of the cat, failed. And, by the time they finally arrived at the Wharton place, Cory's hands hurt from clenching them.

A flurry of activity met them in the Wharton yard. Greg's truck, with Annie, pulled in behind them as they parked the Jeep and got out.

Greetings were brief and painful with the strain of fear and worry surrounding the group of friends. Standing pale and miserable on the lawn by the house, Doris explained the situation, struggling to hold back her tears as the reality of the situation overwhelmed her. She was in the middle of justifying her decision to allow Jenny to bring the boys their lunch when Cory and his dad joined the group.

"We hadn't seen any cougar prints, other than Cory's pictures, and that was so long ago, that…I thought…it was safe…for Jenny to bring lunch…to the boys. But when she hadn't arrived by one thirty, the boys came home. She would never deliberately keep food from her brothers, and she's familiar with the woods. She couldn't just…be lost. Could she?"

"Of course she could!" Annie said as she pushed her way through the group to throw her arm over Doris' shoulder. "She could also have stepped into a small hole and sprained her ankle, or gotten caught by a little fallen tree," Annie continued with hopeful suggestions.

A quick and subtle glance passed from Alex to Cory to Matt as the thought of the poacher's snare entered their minds at the same time. The possibilities that could actually explain Jenny's absence were getting worse.

Bill Wharton stepped forward and raised his hands to the crowd. "Could I have everyone's attention, please," he said. "Matt tells me that the cougar tracks are real." He paused and looked at his wife in sympathy.

Doris paled at his words and for a moment, appeared ready to loose the control she so obviously was struggling to maintain, but Annie was there at her side and gave her a reassuring squeeze. She was not alone.

With difficulty, Bill Wharton divided the searchers and assigned each group to a specific section of the area from his place to Annie's and between the east logging road and the west, an approximate ninety-six square miles—a figure no one mentioned, but of which all of them were aware. Everyone was to converge on the area where the boys had been cutting firewood—Jenny's final destination. If they still had not found her, they would reverse the search and fan out from there and continue until they had covered the whole area a second time.

Searching at night would require flashlights, weapons, and other equipment. Everyone was cautioned about the cougar and warned of the possibility of more than one. Despite the fact that both Annie and Doris were deer hunters and knew how to shoot, they were finally convinced that they would be more help if they were home in case Jenny returned or someone found her. They were also asked to contact the sheriff's department and request more help. It was no longer a "maybe" situation. Jenny was missing!

This was a huge area to cover and Cory glanced at the sky and then to his watch. It was already twenty minutes after six in the evening. Only a hour and a half of daylight was left!

"Mrs. Wharton," Cory asked gently when the others started moving to their vehicles. "What is Jenny wearing?"

Doris shivered in the dropping temperature and stared at Cory for a moment, gathering the strength to speak. "Only tennis shoes, shorts, and a T-shirt. It was still hot when she left."

Hurrying to the Jeep Cory and his father discussed the monumental task of searching for Jenny in the dark. The late August temperature was plunging quickly in its normal threat of nightly freezing and she would be quite cold already, and extremely cold by morning.

Michael drove back to the cabin as fast as possible, where they reopened the shed to grab two lengths of strong rope. Cory retrieved the hunting knife in its leather sheath from the top of the kitchen cupboards and when they discovered that the only ammunition that remained after their summer of shooting practice was a handful of .22 shells, Michael was elected to carry the rifle, a less formidable weapon against the cougar than the shotgun, but better than the hunting knife. Cory added a blanket to his backpack and some food and water. Except for their weapons, he and his father each carried separate and equal supplies in case they lost track of each other.

Glancing at the thermometer attached to the cabin's siding as they stepped out the door, Cory noted that it was already down to fifty-one degrees. Hurrying toward the north, they systematically planned to cover the northern part of their assigned section, starting at the west logging road and heading east. Cory and his father would fan out from each other just far enough to still be able to stay in contact by shouting.

Cory had not voiced his disagreement with the division and method of searching for Jenny. His gut reaction told him that she would be somewhere between their creek and the Wharton property and the area the boys were gathering wood. But who was HE to tell the Whartons how to search for their daughter?

Once out on the logging road, they checked their watches and agreed to meet in exactly one hour. Every few minutes they would make contact by shouting Jenny's name. With flashlights turned on, they started to separate when Michael cautioned his son.

"Cory, be careful!" he said. "This is dangerous for EVERYONE!"

"I know, Dad, but Jenny's in more than one danger, and she might already be seriously hurt."

Michael nodded and they turned their separate ways—Cory to the north of his father.

As familiar as Cory was with the part of the national forest that encompassed their cabin, everything changed at night and nothing looked like it did during the day. Then, too, they weren't sticking to the many trails that he had forged over the summer. They were plowing through the thickness of the woods. Pushing aside the saplings and struggling through the summer's growth of shrubs, grass, and brush, Cory plunged ahead, sweeping his flashlight in an arc, looking for any signs of tracks or blood.

The thought of finding Jenny's blood made Cory shiver despite the heat he was generating by his rapid push through the woods. Fear for her drove him forward and his imagination tormented him with pictures of her lying injured and dying in the cold night air. Each time he called out her name he heard the echo to his right, coming from his father.

In kindness, a full moon had risen at eight-thirty, throwing ghost-like shadows everywhere he looked. However, it was now bright enough to pick one's way without a flashlight, except to prevent the occasional misstep, and Cory turned it off as he approached his father. This was their second meeting since the start of the search.

"See anything?" Cory asked hopefully.

"Nothing," his father answered with a shake of his head.

"Dad, I don't think we're going about this in the right way," Cory complained. "We ought to be starting the search with the cougar prints at our place and working in the direction of the cat."

"Are you THAT sure, Cory, that the cougar is the reason for Jenny being missing?" his father asked. "What if she just wandered off somewhere and hurt herself? Maybe it has nothing to do with the cat."

"Jenny isn't the kind of girl to just wander off," Cory said defensively. "She's smart and responsible. She would NOT have just wandered off or been distracted like a little kid."

Cory knew his fear and anxiety were distorting his common sense, but in the past, he had often relied on his instincts, and right now they were telling him that searching this area was a waste of time. He wiped the sweat from his face and pushed his thick blond hair off his forehead. Despite the cold, damp air, they had been walking hard and Cory couldn't help thinking of Jenny in shorts and a T-shirt. He hoped that she was able to move to keep herself warm.

"I don't know, Dad," he finally answered. "I just know when something feels right and when something is wrong. And this feels very wrong."

They each took a drink of water and checked their flashlights. Extra batteries were in their packs, but when they were traveling over solid open ground, they shut off the lights to conserve the energy.

"We'll hate ourselves if we abandon this area and Jenny is near and hoping to be rescued," Michael pointed out to him.

"I know," Cory conceded, as he picked up his pack and threw it on his back already striding off in his assigned direction.

The moon was now high overhead, removing many of the shadows that had been distorting everything in view. Cory checked his watch as he continued his push through the woods calling Jenny's name over and over again. It was past midnight, and the breath from Cory's strenuous searching, came from his lips in puffs of white clouds. It was COLD! Just how cold, he didn't even want to know.

At two o'clock in the morning they had been searching for six hours and the constant hiking, up rises and down, through swampy areas and over fallen trees, was stealing the energy from their bodies. Converging once more, Cory again expressed his thoughts about the area of their search.

"We only have one more section to sweep and we should be in sight of our cabin," his father explained wisely. "Then, we'll do as you suggest and start our search at the creek."

Cory felt better with those encouraging words and he continued walking without a break. He tried to remember when he had eaten last and thought of the food he carried, but Jenny would need it more than he did and it stayed where it was.

Each time he shouted Jenny's name he waited for a soft cry or whimper in the dark, but the only thing he heard was the return call of her name by his father a distance away from him. And, each time there was nothing, he recited a short prayer for her safety.

The calling out of Jenny's name served two purposes. First, it might reach Jenny and prompt her to signal them in some way. Second, it kept Cory and his father in touch with each other. When the sound of Jenny's name was weak, they knew to move slightly toward the other as they fanned out in their search. However, as the night wore on, they questioned the wisdom of constantly shouting. Finally they agreed that when one of them did not return the call, it signaled that the other might have the cougar in sight and could not risk calling. In that case both would stop shouting and attempt to come together.

In spite of the heat that Cory's body generated with his constant movement, he was aware at all times of the plunging temperature. His breath appeared as frosty air every time the name of Jenny rang out from his lips. She was dressed for the heat of yesterday's noon when temperatures were close to ninety degrees. Now she would be suffering the effects of the cold—that is, if she was still conscious. Mentally, Cory scolded himself for even thinking this way. He needed to think positively, that she would be safe and warm, maybe in a cave somewhere, protected from the elements.

Throughout the night they kept in touch with the Whartons by cell phone, however sporadic that might be, since there were particular spots when service was good and clear and at other times, the best they could hope for would be a quick one-or-two-word message. Perhaps the openness at the cabin or its elevation were key ingredients for reception, because it was one of the best spots for cell phone communication.

They arrived at their cabin at four-thirty in the morning when just a hint of light in the east suggested that morning would follow. Cory and his father had been searching all night and found no sign of Jenny, but they had no intention of quitting. A short break gave them the opportunity to grab something to eat on the way and replenish their water supply, taking only five minutes out of their search. This simple act refreshed Cory's disposition and he struck out for the creek with renewed enthusiasm and a positive attitude.

Steam rose off the water of the creek like a giant airborne snake, marking the path of the stream in both directions as Cory and his father arrived to check for new cat prints in the soft mud along the edge. Although sunrise was not for another hour and a half, the sky was already getting lighter in the east.

"I don't see any new cat prints, just those from yesterday," his father commented after pulling aside the reeds in several places.

Cory wasn't listening. He was watching the steam to see if it was frosting the grass and leaves. He had deliberately not checked the temperature at the cabin for fear of confirming that it had reached freezing. Now, he wished he had looked.

"Dad, did you see what the temperature was when we were at the cabin?"

"It was thirty-six, Cory."

Why did he ask? It was a foolish question and only sent his fears sky-rocketing. If Jenny was hurt, hypothermia would have set in long ago and would kill her by morning, providing the cat hadn't already attacked her. Cory's senses reeled with concern for her.

Pointing directly toward the south, he spoke hurriedly. "Dad, let's fan out from here. You go to the west and I'll go to the east, circling to come out at the lake. I'll meet you at the dock."

The words were barely out of his mouth and he was already across the creek and striding off to the east. Cory was looking for more than blood. Jenny had been carrying lunch to her brothers and, knowing how the three older boys could eat, she would have been carrying quite a large basket of food, enough to satisfy a hungry cougar. If Jenny had the good sense not to run, she might have been able to throw food to the cougar and distract him long enough for her to get away to a safe place where it couldn't reach her. In desperation, Cory tried to hang onto any explanation that was both plausible and hopeful.

Once again, he struggled through the thick brush and broke new trails in an arc from the creek to the lake, assuming the cougar would not have traveled on the same trails that Cory had made throughout the summer, since they were shy creatures and normally avoided people.

Catching a glimpse of the sun through the trees as it peaked above the horizon, Cory headed toward a small ravine near a deposit of large boulders. There between two of the huge rocks something was shining. With branches tearing at his clothes, he broke through an area of scrub oak and hurried to the spot where he thought he had seen a flash of light.

When he reached the place, he scanned the ground, having lost the exact position where he was sure he had caught a reflection. Then glancing up, he spied the object. On one of the boulders, was a small piece of aluminum foil with a smear of what was certainly mustard from the Wharton brother's lunch that Jenny was carrying.

Cory's hands shook as he folded the evidence and pushed it into his pocket. Frantically searching the area, he found nothing else. However, the tiny piece in his pocket gave him hope that Jenny had fed the cougar and escaped. As he attempted a wider search in a circle a distance away from the boulders, he discovered two more pieces of evidence—a small plastic bag of raw vegetables and an orange—neither of which had been eaten or even gnawed.

Eagerly, Cory resumed his search, constantly watching the ground and glancing around himself as he pushed his way toward the lake where he would meet his dad. The nearer he came to the lake, the more scraps of aluminum he found and by the time he climbed the small hill to descend to the lake he was almost running.

His father was pacing at the dock when Cory arrived and they quickly compared notes and planned the next segment of their search. Both agreed that the cougar was most likely the reason for Jenny's absence, and both were anxious to start out again.

Suggesting that he cover the lake area by starting on the west shore and circling to the east, Michael was about to leave when he gripped Cory's shoulder and looked intently at him. "Don't be a hero, son," he said. "I wish you'd give me the knife and take the rifle."

Cory shook his head. "The knife has already saved one life this summer, Dad. I feel safer with it than I do with the rifle." He paused at the questioning look on his father's face. "Someday I'll tell you the story. For now, just trust me."

With that, he turned and ran up the hill toward the northeast. He was glad his father had chosen the lake area to search, leaving Cory the one area that he was more convinced would prove successful. As he moved along, he checked his watch. It was eight o'clock in the morning. This should be the time for Jenny to be eating breakfast in a warm home, surrounded by family, instead of being cold and alone. He increased his pace and the search went on.

Chapter 16

It was a clear morning and if there was anything good to say about the day, it was that it was warming rapidly and Cory held on to that thought as he zigzagged back and forth through the trees. As the temperature continued to rise with the sun, he released his pack from his back and stored his jacket and flashlight inside, then, resumed his search.

He had skirted the swamp near the lake and was now entering a plantation of tall pines. Under normal circumstances, this would be one of his favorite spots. Void of any brush, the area of fallen pine needles formed a thick carpet between the towering trees. Cory loved everything about the pines, from the sweet smell of the green needles to the crunch of brown ones under his feet, and the sound of the wind as it rushed softly through the boughs. But today was different and he had no time to enjoy the gifts of nature.

While he wound his way through the plantation, he came upon some important evidence quite by accident. About twenty feet to his left, the bed of pine needles on the floor of the forest appeared to have been swept aside as though someone or something had been clearing an area. Quickly investigating, Cory found cougar scat littering the spot, causing him to question, once more, the number of cougars roaming the woods.

Knowing about the cautious and stealthy movements for which the cat was noted, Cory kept glancing in a wide circle to prevent a sudden attack. Following his instincts, he stopped calling out Jenny's name and placed his backpack against the side of a tree, removing the rope and tying it around his waist. He wanted freedom of movement for himself and unconsciously his right hand went to the knife, making sure it was there. The cat was near. He was sure of that!

Silently and slowly, Cory moved toward the edge of the plantation where the terrain changed to heavy brush and small poplars, crowded close to each other. Here it was harder to walk without being heard, but he was grateful that he was downwind from his direction of travel. Hopefully the cougar was somewhere in front of him.

With barely perceptible steps, he cautiously headed toward a large outcropping of glacially deposited rock that he could just make out beyond the poplars. Cougars in the southwest were commonly found lying on mountain rock ledges and every ounce of intuition told Cory that this was where a cougar would be found. Pushing aside the nagging thoughts that said he was placing too much trust in his instincts, he worked his way forward to get a clearer look.

The top of the outcropping was at least twenty-five feet high and ran horizontally for about a hundred feet before dirt and growth covered it as it sloped suddenly downward. Cory was now inching forward and already crouching as low as possible with soundless movement. Constantly sweeping his gaze in the hope that he would see the cat before it saw him, his eyes suddenly froze on one spot. The front edge of the outcropping that faced him was a blunt drop with a small narrow ledge about twelve or fourteen feet up from the ground. On the ledge was a spot of red—bright red!

"Wait! Don't run!" his mind shouted at him. "Move slowly and see what it is."

It took every ounce of will power to keep from jumping up and hollering Jenny's name and running to see if it was her. Instead, Cory slid closer to the ground and moved forward silently until he was close enough to see clearly.

It WAS Jenny! Cory's reflexes started to bring him to his feet when a slight movement on the top of the huge rock pushed him to the ground. The cougar was lying on the very top as though sunning himself—or waiting! It was the casual flick of the tail that Cory had seen from the corner of his eye. By staying tight against the ground Cory could see the ledge but not the cougar, and he studied the situation.

Jenny was lying on the narrow ledge and, if not for the one arm flung to the side and her awkward position, Cory would have guessed that she was sleeping. Instead, he suspected that she was unconscious.

Where was his dad and how could he warn his father to sneak up quietly? Cory hugged the ground, trying to decide what to do.

As he examined the rock formation more closely, he realized that the cougar must be aware of Jenny but could not get to her. The only way that Cory could explain her presence on the ledge was that she had come from the top and tried to lower herself over the edge and fell. The rock above her head was rounded so much that once on the ledge she could never get off without dropping downward to the ground. However, the drop down onto the sharp, irregular rock edges from twelve or fourteen feet would certainly cause serious injury, if not death.

Suddenly the cat got up and padded over to peer over the edge at Jenny, proving Cory's reasoning. Lying down, the cougar stretched one paw over the rock as far as possible toward the prey he couldn't reach. A grumble seemed to roll from its throat as it stood up and began pacing along the top of the outcropping.

Cory could wait no longer. Time was slipping away. If Jenny is hurt, she could be dying. Maybe his father won't be here for hours. Something has to be done NOW!

Slipping the knife from its sheath, he planned his moves and watched the constant pacing of the cougar. Each time the cat turned away from him, Cory made a quick and silent move toward the outcropping.

It was noon with the warmth of a high sun and suddenly NO wind. The chance that the cat would get a whiff of another human scent was extremely possible, and Cory knew that he might have to deal with the cat sooner than he hoped to. If he could get to the ledge that Jenny was lying on, he could at least see if she was hurt. From that position the cat couldn't reach HIM either and from there, Cory could attempt to call others by cell phone or shouting or screaming—whatever worked.

Pressing his back flat against the wall of the outcropping, Cory slowly moved sideways along the rock. This position kept him as close to the rock as possible and hopefully out of the vision of the cougar. In order to reach Jenny, Cory was banking on a small, sharp chunk of rock that split and hung away from the original rock halfway up the cliff above Jenny. If he could lasso it, he could pull himself up to the ledge.

Releasing the rope that he had tied to his waist, however, brought his body slightly away from the rock and the cougar spied him. As the cat flexed his huge body for a leaping attack, Cory rushed away from the wall where he would have had no chance to defend himself. Reaching the grass covered ground a few feet from the rock, he spun around and held the hunting knife out in front of him, knowing the claws would strike him first and then the teeth would sink into his throat.

Cory had one chance and that was to plunge his knife from the throat of the cat upward into the head. As the huge cat made a flying leap from the rock, Cory steeled himself for the blow of the claws and at the last moment he joined his left hand to his right around the handle of the huge hunting knife, stiffening his arms.

Everything came together in one terrible moment as the claws of the cat ripped into his shoulders and the extreme weight crushed him to the ground. Rolling to the side as the tremendous weight of the cougar fell on him, Cory withdrew the knife that had hit its mark and was prepared to plunge it into the cat again, when he was stopped by hands that grabbed him.

In a daze, he turned to find his father and Matt, who took the knife from his hands and forced him to sit down.

Suddenly there were other voices all talking at once and Cory had to shake himself to clear his head. Looking around, he realized that the cougar was dead and lying on the ground next to him, and it was the sensation of wetness rather than the pain that informed him that blood was running down his arms. Then, he remembered Jenny!

"Sit still!" his father ordered as he tried to remove Cory's bloody shirt after signaling to the others that his son was all right.

"Jenny!"

"They're getting her off the ledge now."

While his father wrapped bandages over the claw marks on both of his shoulders to staunch the bleeding, Cory watched the flurry of activity. He heard the concern and fear as they gently lowered Jenny from the rock ledge and placed her on a litter. Two men with paramedic uniforms on, checked her pulse and vital signs, then signaled the others to pick up the litter. Mr. Wharton, with fear and worry etched on his face, stood helplessly aside as the others did what they were trained to do, and all five of Jenny's brothers, along with a few neighbors, followed the men as they carried the litter toward the closest logging road. When Mr. Wharton turned toward Cory,

Michael waved him on.

"We're fine here, Bill," he said. "Take care of your daughter."

They received a nod, a fleeting smile with a look of gratitude, and a wave from Jenny's father as he hurried after the litter

"Is Jenny going to be okay?" Cory asked as he got unsteadily to his feet.

It was an unanswerable question.

The claw marks on Cory's shoulders were deep but non-threatening. The cougar had struck the muscle of his arms and not a major vein or artery, but he felt the burn of the slashed cuts and the weakness of his arms from the weight of the falling cat. The trip back to the cabin was slow and tiresome. Cory had no more energy. In the past twenty-four hours he had eaten little and slept even less.

Michael carried both backpacks and the rifle while they trekked back to the cabin for the Jeep. A trip to the hospital was necessary. Cory's wounds would need some stitching and checking on Jenny would come automatically.

Dropping the gear on the porch, Michael retrieved a fresh shirt from the cabin and they immediately hopped into the Jeep. They would check to see who might still be at the Wharton place before heading to Woodville, although they were sure that everyone would be gone by now.

When Cory had chosen to reach Jenny without waiting for help, he didn't know that all the searchers were converging on that spot. It wasn't discovered until midmorning that a one-square-mile of woods, bordering each of the divided search areas, had inadvertently been missed by every search team, and that was exactly where Jenny was. The timing had been perfect.

Although Cory was exhausted, his concern for Jenny and the constant replaying in his mind of the events of the last few hours kept him awake on the long drive to Woodville. As they expected, the Wharton place was devoid of humans when they arrived. Annie must have gone with Doris when they received the news about Jenny which explained the absence of vehicles in their yard. With that fact confirmed, Michael smoothly swung the Jeep in a circle and turned down the driveway back to the blacktop road that would bring them to the hospital.

Today was Wednesday, the day they were leaving the cabin to go home. With that thought came the realization that Jenny didn't know that Cory was coming back here to live with Annie for the winter and attend Woodville High. He couldn't wait to tell her. A million questions swept into his mind. Was she okay? If it was a blow to the head that made her unconscious, wouldn't she have come around by now? Could this be more serious? Was it possible that she would have permanent damage? Cory didn't want to think of these depressing possibilities.

Pushing the thoughts of Jenny aside, Cory concentrated on the cougar and suddenly he realized that they still didn't know if there was more than one cat or not. Before they left the scene of Jenny's rescue, he had studied the size and features of the cougar. Everyone had been right. No cougars lived in the northern forests of this state, at least, not until now. Where had it come from? How did it get here? Was there a mate?

While the Jeep roared down the highway, Cory shifted his thoughts once more.

"Dad, were you ever trained as a sniper? Like in the army or something?" he asked with a grin.

"I don't think so," his dad answered laughingly. "I think I would have remembered that."

"Although you only had the little twenty-two caliber

rifle, it would have killed the cat if you shot it between and just above the eyes, wouldn't it?

"Yes. I'm sure it would. Why?"

"Well, I was just wondering who killed it," Cory reflected half to himself. "Did you, with your perfect shot, or did I with my knife?"

His father looked over at Cory and grinned. "I guess we'll never really know. Does it matter?"

Cory shrugged. "I was just wondering if my knife could have killed it if you hadn't shot. Don't get me wrong. I'm grateful you shot. I was just wondering if the knife and the position could have done it."

"Your knife has a twelve inch blade on it, Cory, and you sent it through the throat and into the brain. The cat was dead whether I shot or not."

Satisfied with the answer, Cory relaxed against the back of the seat and rode the rest of the way with his eyes closed, silently praying that Jenny would be all right.

In the emergency room of the Woodville Hospital, his wounds were cleaned, stitched, and bandaged by a young intern not much older than Cory.

"If it was my choice," he said to them, "you'd be given a bed and kept overnight, but we are full at the moment. Until they expand this hospital, we're often full." Turning to Michael he continued. "Get him home and into bed. A good night's rest and plenty of fluids to allow his body to replace the blood that he's lost will help. The stitches come out in about a week."

Annie rushed into the emergency room just as they were being dismissed and pelted them with questions. She was alarmed by the bandages she saw peeking from Cory's shirt and she checked Michael over from head to foot. It took a few moments to quiet her enough to ask about Jenny.

"Grandmother, I'm fine, but please tell me about

Jenny," Cory pleaded. "Is she okay?"

Annie's incredibly blue eyes always told the truth, and they spelled worry now, as she hesitated in her answer. "They really can't tell too much yet, Cory. Jenny is still unconscious. They've done a brain scan and the doctor suspects that it might be only a mild concussion but until she's awake, they're not sure."

On the second floor of the hospital they found the Wharton family quietly huddled at the end of the hallway. As they approached, Cory couldn't help feeling the dread that seemed to be hanging over the whole family. He nodded with a small smile to acknowledge each of them and accepted the gratitude expressed by Bill and Doris for his part in the search and rescue. Doris' mothering instincts matched Annie's and Cory was obliged to answer, once more, the thousand and one questions about his health and wounds.

Like sheep they filed into a tiny waiting room and filled the sofas that lined the walls and flopped into the beanbag chairs that were spread around the floor. It was a quiet group that assembled to wait. Cory had never seen Jenny's brothers so subdued. Periodically, either Bill or Doris went to Jenny's room to sit and wait for their daughter to regain consciousness. The minutes on the clock dragged into hours and conversations came to a halt. The waiting seemed endless.

As evening approached, Michael's argument that they return to the cabin, won with the help of Annie and Jenny's parents. They convinced Cory that he was not contributing anything by just sitting and waiting, and in the mean time, his health was at risk. He didn't have to like it, but they were right, and he finally agreed to leave.

"Promise me that you'll call the moment Jenny wakes up," Cory begged when Bill Wharton walked them down the hallway, again praising them for their part in the rescue.

"If I can't reach you on the cell phone, I'll send one of the boys to let you know. I promise," he said.

Michael ran the Jeep through the first fast-food place he saw before leaving Woodville and ordered a frighteningly unhealthy sack full of malts, cheeseburgers, and fries. It wasn't until his father pulled in to order and the smells of the food reached Cory that he realized how famished he was. In more than a day, they had each eaten only one carelessly thrown together sandwich. In less than fifteen minutes, Cory consumed two cheeseburgers, half the fries and one of the malts, while his father drove. Switching places, Michael wolfed down the remainder while the Jeep roared back to the cabin.

Sleep was the magic word and it came without effort. Backpacks and the rifle had been pulled into the cabin from the porch and left lying on the floor next to the still bloody knife. They would deal with the cleanup tomorrow. Despite Cory's worry about Jenny, his exhaustion overpowered him and his sleep was deep and replenishing.

The contrary weather sent warm southerly breezes northward throughout the night and when Cory woke, the early morning temperatures were in the sixties, foretelling a hot and muggy end of summer vacation. Flexing his arms to relieve the stiff and sore muscles, he joined his father in closing up the cabin for the season. There was little food for breakfast and because they were eager to check on Jenny, they planned to catch a meal in town.

Reluctantly, Cory had agreed to leave this morning whether Jenny had regained consciousness or not. His father gave him no choice in the matter. They needed to get home to organize Cory's return to Woodville and

Michael had been away from his work for too long already.

With the Jeep packed to overflowing and everything at the cabin stored and locked, they drove down the familiar ruts to the logging road. Cory looked back one last time and thought about the wonderful summer he had enjoyed.

"We have five hundred miles to drive today, Cory," his father reminded him, "and I expect a detailed explanation of the hunting knife. You know, the one that had already saved one life, before saving yours?"

Cory grinned and nodded, hoping that the telling of the story would not prevent him from ever returning to the cabin he loved. "Later, Dad," he promised. "You're right. We have a long ride ahead of us and plenty of time."

It was not a good sign that no one had called them during the night. They could only assume that Jenny was still unconscious. If it was a simple concussion, wouldn't she be awake by now? With renewed energy all the worries and concerns for Jenny came back to Cory, stronger than ever. He pushed the thought of permanent mental damage to the back of his mind every time it surfaced, but with each passing hour the idea reinforced itself and panicked him.

They arrived at the hospital's second floor lounge to find a discouraged and subdued family. Throughout the night they had taken turns sitting with Jenny and going home to clean up, grab a little sleep, and eat whether they wanted to or not. Jenny's condition had not changed although the doctor still insisted that she had no other injuries and could wake at any time.

When Michael explained that they were forced to leave this morning, Doris suggested that Cory might want to sit with Jenny for a few minutes, and to his surprise, she also thought he should play his guitar for her.

"She has always loved music, Cory," Doris explained, "and the doctor said we should try talking to her or bringing her things that might stir her subconscious." Tears filled her eyes as she added. "We have nothing to lose."

Michael agreed and hurried back to the Jeep for the guitar.

Cautiously Cory pushed the heavy door inward and entered the austere and sterile hospital room. They were typically all the same—one bed, one chair, one light, one window, and the undefined smell of illness.

Jenny looked small and vulnerable, lying with her forehead wrapped in bandages and her eyes closed. Cory felt a physical pain of sadness as he looked at her. Even unconscious, she was beautiful.

Quietly he moved the single chair over to the bed to be close to her. He positioned the guitar and began to play a soft and soothing melody. It was a beautiful love song and although he NEVER sang, he liked the words and began to sing it softly. As usual, Cory's music took over his senses and soon his eyes had closed and all he heard was the melody floating in the air. He moved from one piece of music to the next as quietly as he could. So engrossed was he that it took more than a moment to recognize the sound of another.

"Monsieur, do you have permission to be in my room?" a weak voice asked him.

Cory's eyes flew open and his hands froze in position. The grin he saw and the beautiful open eyes spread a smile across his face.

"Oui, Mademoiselle. I am just your local Jester, here to entertain you," he said.

They couldn't stop grinning at each other and then

a deep frown formed on Jenny's face.

"I don't remember how I got here," she said. "I just remember the cougar…Oh, Cory," she whispered, "your cougar is real!"

"Shh, I know!" he said. "Don't speak! You need to save your strength and I need to tell your family that you're awake."

"Wait!" she cried weakly. "Cory, come here."

He moved back to the edge of the bed.

"You're hurt!" she exclaimed, spying the bandages sticking out of his shirt.

"You are too," he responded as he turned to leave.

"Don't you dare leave without telling me how you got hurt," she demanded.

The real Jenny is back, Cory thought.

At the door, he turned and answered. "I'll tell you next time I see you."

"I'm not waiting 'til Christmas to hear the story!"

"Actually, it will be Monday," Cory answered with a grin. "See you at school," he threw over his shoulder as he let the door swing shut behind him.

"She's awake," he said unnecessarily to the family members rushing to the door.

Cory and his dad walked down the hallway and headed for the Jeep. What a GREAT summer this has been he thought. And he couldn't help the slight swagger that crept into his walk as they left the hospital.

The End